ALL WINDOWS OPEN

and other stories

ALL WINDOWS OPEN

and other stories

HARIKLIA HERISTANIDIS

Clouds of Magellan | Melbourne

Clouds of Magellan Publishing

www.cloudsofmagellan.net

Melbourne, Australia

National Library of Australia Cataloguing-in-Publication entry

Heristanidis, Hariklia

All windows open : and other stories

ISBN 978-0-646-57794-4 (PBK)

823.4

Cover image – Hariklia Heristanidis

Cover design – Gordon Thompson

Dedicated to the two Alexandras

Contents

All Windows Open

It is only with the heart that one can see rightly;
what is essential is invisible to the eye.

The Little Prince, Antoine de Saint-Exupery

My name is Chrissie Triantafillou and I am a shallow person. I judge on appearances and gravitate to the beautiful. Believe me when I say I could never be friends with anyone who had a mole on their face. I simply cannot live with that kind of stress. Dandruff repulses me, crooked teeth frighten me and don't get me started on superfluous facial hair. I attribute this personality trait to a childhood illness that left me without a sense of smell. From that time on I lived as if on a veneer, where surface was everything. I knew nothing of things hidden, of depth and intuition. Or so it was until George's return.

I met my cousin George twice. First as a newborn girl, on an unremarkable summer day in 1960; and then again, as a woman in her twenties at Melbourne airport, in 1985. Our first meeting is a forgotten moment. Our second is etched into my brain like a scar.

I had gone to the airport with his family: my mother's brother (Uncle Nick), his wife (Aunt Eleni) and their daughter, George's sister Tina. George was returning home after three years of travelling around Europe, teaching English, and I couldn't wait to see him.

We had grown up together, like siblings; slept in the same bed during sleepovers, shared confidences, scraped knees and germs on mercurochrome drenched cotton balls. But when George walked through the arrival gates, standing upright despite his enormous backpack, he was clearly not the same person. How else to explain the chiselled cleft in his chin and the way his hair curled over his collar? I wanted to run my fingers through his hair and my tongue across the stubble on his chin. In an instant my whole notion of right and wrong turned, like milk souring in the sun.

My parents were not particularly concerned about my olfactory limitations until the time I almost blew up the house. Before that, I believe they thought my only problem was a tendency to be vague.

I was fourteen and recovering from a severe cold, when I was left home alone while my mother called on one of the neighbours. 'Watch the lentils,' she said before leaving the house, 'I won't be long.' She was planning to make them into a thick brown soup called *fuk-yes*, a name all us Greek kids at school found endlessly funny.

As soon as I was sure she'd gone, I switched on the telly and settled back on the couch to watch *The Young and The Restless*. Within minutes the vertical hold of our set lost its tenuous grip. Cursing my bad luck I rushed to fix the flickering image, reaching behind the set, straining to find the dials my father used to steady the black and white picture. I had forgotten all about the lentils, which had boiled over and extinguished the flame of the cooker. Gas flowed into our kitchen and throughout the house, as I settled back to watch Snapper visit his ex-girlfriend Chris. I was hoping they would get back together. I was already a sucker for a good love story.

'Chrissie!' my mother screamed upon opening the back door. I quickly turned off the telly. What had I done, or not done? Oh yes, the lentils. She tore into the living room opening the window and waving a tea towel in the air. It reminded me of the frantic waving of white handkerchiefs during Greek dancing. Then she crossed herself over and over. 'Sweet Jesus, mother of God, saints above.' I hadn't realised that the consistency of the lentils was of such acute importance. 'What are you doing, you silly girl!' I felt her hand across the back of my head, 'stupid donkey.' Insults from her home village. 'Thank God your father wasn't with me. His cigarette …' She crossed herself again, then squeezed me tightly against her enormous bosom.

Not long after, my mother made an appointment with a specialist. He said I had an olfactory disorder called 'anosmia', from the Greek, naturally, meaning *no smell*. My parents' language seemed to be responsible for many of the world's diseases. The doctor said there was no cure.

My mother Voula tells me of a dream she had when she was pregnant. 'My grandmother, your great grandmother, came to me in a dream. In the dream she gave me a pair of gold earrings. A gift of earrings means a girl. If it had been a gift of a cross on a chain, it would have meant a boy. I didn't even know I was pregnant with you. Your father and I had only been married a month.' We are sitting in bed, feasting on bread drizzled with olive oil and ripe tomatoes from our garden, which we bite into like apples. My father Vasili is working late in his barber shop. I am eight and Mum is twenty-six. We are two girls telling secrets in the dark. After eating we shake out the crumbs and Mum tucks me into bed with a kiss.

That was before my anosmia. Afterwards, with no sense of smell, when my appetite shrunk to that of a sparrow, I tried my mother's patience. So much so that she was driven to putting a curse on me. 'May you have a child that causes you as much difficulty as you've caused me.' In most stories, curses are the domain of stepmothers or evil fairies. But if the hospital records are to be believed, it was my actual biological mother who was driven to such fairy tale behaviour. It appears to be true, I was a difficult child. Aunt Eleni, George's mother, backs up Mum's version of events. 'You were such a fussy eater!' she says. 'You drove your mother mad with worry.' I agree with the mad part.

Eating was a mechanical thing for me, like going to the toilet. It brought me no pleasure. Food was simply a series of textures. Chicken was little different from steak, and except for the colour, mash potato was indistinguishable from mashed pumpkin. I dreaded meal times. Lunch was a battle, dinner time a war. Once a conduit for conversation, food was now a source of isolation. I spent hours alone at the kitchen table. 'You are not moving until that plate is empty, my girl.' Then at other times there was wild activity; blurred figures around the Hills Hoist. 'Come back here and have this last mouthful,' my mother would yell, apron flying, arm outstretched like she was competing in an egg and spoon race. I was thin as a whippet and just as fast. My reputation as a difficult child was set.

I hear my mother's voice now as it echoes from the past, 'A mother's curse always sticks. A mother's curse will always come true!' Perhaps it's a Greek thing: mother's curses. Greek mythology is after all a series of stories about dysfunctional families. Fathers who believe they are gods, mothers who outwit them, mixed up progeny that are half god, half mortal, questions of paternity, elopements, death and retribution: much the same as any soap on television. The air I breathed in inner city Melbourne in the 1960s was not only loaded with lead from car exhaust fumes, but also with fables, dreams, fortune telling and curses.

As it turned out, my mother's curse loomed over my life, but never really bloomed; although for a time I believed it had ruined everything. That was when I found myself unexpectedly pregnant and carrying a deformed being, a monster rather than a baby. Or so I suspected. But I'm getting ahead of myself.

Hope

My name is Magdalena Mavros and I am known throughout this neighbourhood of Little Greece as the widow on the corner. To say the truth it's more of a united nations around here. We have some Italians, a Croatian or two and naturally the Pommies and Australians, who to us are the same thing. Me, I am with the Greeks. Part of and apart, for I am a private person. I don't mind my widow's label, and the fact that no one sees the person beneath the black clothing that I'm required to wear. I keep a professional distance from the women who come to see me for hope and gossip. I am not their friend.

I can lift an evil eye curse, but mostly I read coffee cups. I learned to do this at my grandmother's knee, back in Greece. She was known for having this gift throughout our town and to the villages beyond. *Yiayia* was very clever; she taught me to read not only the symbols in the cups but the faces of the people who came to see her, women mostly. Women looking for something that was often right in front of them. It's a good thing for me that most people cannot see beyond their very noses. There'd be no call for my coffee cup readings if they could. *Yiayia* was also a young widow but she was never short of fresh vegetables and we ate chicken more than most people in the town. She made a good living from her gift, as I do. Together with what Stavros left me, God rest his soul, I am living well in this lucky country.

In the car on the way home from the airport, I was acutely aware of the physicality of George. He sat in the middle of the back seat, with myself and Tina on either side: a thorn between the roses. My surname, Triantafillou actually means 'rose' in Greek. I glanced down and noticed the bulk of his thigh next to mine, the masculine curve; and I felt the muscle of his arm rubbing against my shoulder. The dark stubble on his face was driving me nuts. I'd never thought of tiny bits of hair having such a strong sexual hold. Much as I wanted to lean over and snuggle against him, I sat up straight, fighting the new feelings I had. Their sudden appearance and intensity was frightening me. I already had a boyfriend and besides, relations between first cousins are strictly taboo in Greek society. The Orthodox Church won't marry first cousins. It's like falling in love with your brother.

Five minutes out of the airport car park, George shuffled in his seat and said, 'I wanted to wait until we were back home to tell you all, but I can't hold it back any longer.' I turned my head to look at him. Could it be he felt it too? 'I'm in love.' My heart pounded so hard I thought everyone in the car would hear it.

Aunt Eleni turned her head and peered over the front seat, her eyes were still red from all the crying she'd done at the arrival gate. Uncle Nick glanced into the rear view mirror, Tina raised her eyebrows, I held my breath. 'Her name is Dora. I met her in a café in Thessaloniki.'

No one said a word. 'We've been inseparable for the last month and as soon as she can get her residency papers sorted out, we're going to be married.'

I grew up in Thornbury, in Melbourne's inner north, on a wide treeless street with deep bluestone gutters. Nature strips were for those who lived on the other side of the Yarra. Although I was an only child, I grew up with my cousins George and Tina, who lived three doors up from our house. They were first cousins, next best to actual siblings. Greek relationships are strictly hierarchical: ties of blood are everything. On the family tree my cousins and I were like adjacent olive branches, always rubbing together.

In those hazy childhood days it seemed like every weekend was either Christmas, Easter or a someone's name day. There was always an excuse to get together, to prepare food and eat. Afterwards Dad and Uncle Nick would sit back and smoke, while Mum and Aunt Eleni did the dishes. George, Tina and I would go outside and play with the other kids from our street: Trevor the skip, Nick and his sister Val and her friend Katy, and the spaghetti brothers Robert and Tino. We chose teams for cricket or footy depending on the season, or we'd ride our scooters and bikes up and down the black asphalt footpaths at speeds that made our mothers scream.

During the week and on Saturday mornings, my father Vasili worked in his barber shop on High Street, then on Sundays he went to what Mum called 'his church', the *kafenio*, the café. Most of the Greek men went there to drink small cups of coffee and ouzo, to read the Greek papers and to play a little backgammon. Uncle Nick too, was one of the converted. The only genuinely pious member of the family was Aunt Eleni, who dragged George and Tina with her to church to practise Orthodoxy. The word itself means upright or correct. Greeks believe that all things civilised began with them: theatre, mathematics, medicine and God.

We didn't go to church. My mother's true calling was sanitation; and in that, I was her reluctant accomplice. My mother cleaned with a passion most people reserve for religious experiences or true love. Every week, every surface of our entire home was either vacuumed or coated in disinfectant. Mum bought the hospital grade stuff by the ten gallon, from a friend who worked as a cleaner at the local hospital. She splashed it over the concrete floor of our outside toilet and used a hard bristled broom to sweep the liquid into every crevice.

When she said, 'Smells clean', my mother's face had the same look as saints in icons did, flushed and fit for heaven. I was given my own duster at the age of three and was hauling the vacuum cleaner from room to room at nine.

The other big Sunday task at our house was cooking. My mother made large oven trays of *pita*, pastry with various fillings. She made cheese and spinach ones (*spanako-pita*) for savoury meals and others filled with chopped walnuts and drizzled in honey and cinnamon, for sweets. She whizzed pink fish roe in her Sunbeam Mixmaster together with stale bread, olive oil and salt to make *taramasalata*. And she hung muslin bags of yoghurt from the kitchen taps. They dripped cloudy water into the sink. Afterwards the thickened yoghurt was transformed into *tzatziki* with the addition of garlic and grated cucumber. Mum roasted meat in the oven, chicken or lamb, sometimes beef. Salad was assembled from tomatoes and cucumbers grown in our *bak-ze*, veggie garden. And a Greek table would never be complete without feta cheese, bread and olives. I would help in this department too, peeling cucumbers or drying the dishes.

'Smells fantastic in here,' Dad would say, coming home from the *kafenio*. He was always cheerful after an ouzo or two. I didn't have a clue what he meant. In the living room *World Championship Wrestling* would just be starting. Jack Little would announce that it was The Golden Greek, Spiros Arion, versus Mario Milano, the original Italian Stallion. But we had to finish lunch before Mum would let us watch.

My mother's other passion was her garden. Much as she hated dirt inside the house, outside she revelled in the texture of mud and the smell of fertilizer. But if you asked her if gardening was a hobby, she would be quick to say no. A hobby implied spare time. She was a pragmatic woman and only grew things that could be eaten. 'Pragma' means *thing* in Greek. My mother was a matter of fact person. In summer we had tomatoes, cucumbers, green peppers; in winter, beans and pumpkin. And all year round fragrant herbs: parsley, rosemary, mint and basil. A large bay leaf tree dominated the back yard, rivalled only by the Hills Hoist. 'Just smell the basil,' my mother would say, as I helped her hang out the washing. But I wasn't interested in things that were invisible.

I sat on George's bed as he emptied the contents of his backpack onto the shaggy beige carpet of his room. Tina was in the kitchen brewing Greek coffee for the visitors, including my parents who had called in to see George.

'Don't say anything interesting while I'm out,' she said, 'I'll be right back.' But as soon as she left the room George's eyes lit up with excitement.

'Actually I *do* have something else to tell you Chrissie.'

'What? A child as well?'

'No, nothing like that, but it does involve Dora.' This was getting worse and worse. 'We're going into business together, importing a range of trendy Greek cosmetics and toiletries into Australasia.'

Cosmetic products! From a guy who, as far as I knew just washed with soap and water. 'But George, what do you know about cosmetic products?'

'Dora's the one right into all that. I'm in charge of the business end. Did I tell you she's a qualified beautician?'

'No.'

'She knows all about facials and exfoliants.' Exfoliants! Despite an impressive vocabulary, I'd never heard George use that word before. 'It's a range of products made in Greece, really popular and not very expensive. They use all natural ingredients, but their main draw card …' he paused for effect, 'is bee's wax and honey.'

'Honey?'

'Nectar of the Gods.'

'That's overstating it a little isn't it?' I said.

'No, that's the name of our range, *Nectar of the Gods.*' George's voice rose with excitement. 'We're repackaging for the Australian and New Zealand markets. You know, something simple but stylish.'

Perhaps my lustful feelings towards George were rooted in an imperceptible though genuine change in him. In a way, he really did seem like a different person. Where was George the teacher, the conduit of knowledge? Before me now was a man with a fiancé, an entrepreneur who was into money and beauty products. The more my cousin spoke, the more I felt like I was being left behind: still at home, still in the same job, still more-or-less a child. 'I guess I could help with the design and packaging,' I said.

'Well Dora has some ideas already, so we're pretty right on that side of things.' He unzipped one of the side pockets of his backpack and pulled out a brown paper bag, inside were some small cakes of soap, honey coloured.

'Just smell this,' George said holding one up to my nose.

'You know I …'

'Sorry Chrissie. Dumb of me to forget. You'd think I'd been gone for ten years rather than three.' With his eyes closed, he took a big sniff and exhaled dramatically. 'Listen, don't tell your folks or Tina anything about all this just yet. I want to get the ball rolling first. As well as soap, we have lip balm, night and day face creams and even a volumising hair mask.' Oh my God, someone had kidnapped my cousin George and in his place put a gay Greek hairdresser.

'You guys coming to the kitchen?' Tina asked from the doorway. 'Coffee's made.' George got to his feet, grabbing the bag of soap.

'Smell this,' he said to his sister.

'That's lovely,' Tina said.

'I'm glad you like it. I've one for you, one for our cousin here,' he said throwing one gently to me, 'and one for each of the mums.'

'Thank you George, how thoughtful,' said Tina. I didn't know what to say. I felt like I'd been dropped into some kind of labyrinth, and had no idea how to get back.

In some ways life was as it had always been. George was living three doors up, and our families continued to live in each other's pockets. But I was avoiding George and my family as much as possible and spending more time with my boyfriend James, or as I was increasingly thinking of him—the antidote. I was hoping that the less I saw of George, the sooner I would come to my senses and see him the way I always had, as a big brother.

As well laid plans go, it almost worked. During the day I was able to bury the ache I felt to be with George under a list of tasks, meetings and social engagements. But he was always with me, like an undiagnosed disease; the symptoms of which flared up at night, while I lay asleep and powerless. The more I suppressed my longing during the day, the more I dreamed of George at night, when my lascivious unconscious took over. One dream in particular recurred constantly. In this wordless dream I had my cheek pressed against George's face and my fingers through his hair. There was a stillness, an everything rightness in our being together in the dream, that was impossible to recapture during the day. I wanted to grab hold of that dream and pull it with me into my wakefulness. It was the first time since the onset of anosmia that I felt I was missing out on something. I wanted to know George's smell. I wanted to know his taste and feel his lips. I longed to kiss him.

Sometimes, outside of dreaming, I dared to hope that the two of us might get together, despite the cousin thing. But whenever I saw George, all he did was talk about Dora; their late night phone calls and plans for the future.

'Did I tell you she speaks five languages?'

'No.'

'She says the grammatical structure of German is identical to Greek. She picked it up as a child from a German family holidaying in Greece. Isn't that amazing?'

'Yes, impressive.' I found keeping up the fake smile and banal comments, exhausting: 'Really? That's great George.' My God, hadn't he noticed anything was wrong? He wasn't anywhere near as smart as I'd always thought he was. My mother however did notice something amiss.

'Someone has given you the evil eye,' she said. 'We will go and see Mrs Mavros, the widow who lives on the corner. 'Who has been flattering you? Telling you how pretty you are?' She shook her head, 'Some women just don't know any better.' My mother believed unequivocally in the evil eye. It seemed somehow rational to her that a compliment from a jealous person would curse the object of their adoration. The fact that the person placing the curse was almost always female was not so surprising. Our sex has always been linked to the supernatural: just think of Salem and the witches. In Greek circles a bad mood, a feeling of being unwell or a headache is often explained away by the evil eye, which is said to follow a flattering remark. This may have explained why my mother never said anything nice about me.

Love

A young girl from the neighbourhood, Chrissie, came to see me today. What a joy it was to be near someone with their life so open and ahead of them. Her mother Voula brought her to see me. I like Voula, she is a good lady, from a good family. She never tries to squeeze gossip from me, like some of the others. 'Someone has given her the evil eye,' Voula insisted. The child is love sick, plain as day. But I performed the ritual and collected my fee. Oh, the sweet ache of love. I wonder who has possessed her so.

Chrissie's visit reminded me of the afternoon Stavros and I met. It was during the spring after I had finished high school. I was helping out in my aunt's shop, when he came in to buy tobacco. For a week after that first visit I could hardly eat and I remember my own mother blaming the evil eye, and in fairness, isn't love a type of bewitching? Stavros seemed to me like a man, where all the boys from my class were just that, boys. His hair was shiny brown, but his moustache had a ginger tinge, which I found immensely intriguing.

At the time I had been dreaming of getting a place at Aristotle University in Thessaloniki. I wanted to move to a big city and study languages. I wanted to teach. But Stavros pursued me and courted me like I was a princess. I could not hold out against his charm and besides, I had been in love with him from the first moment we met. It was only later that he told me of his plan to go to Australia.

'We will work for five years and make a lot of money,' he said holding my hand as we walked along the edge of the lake in our town. It is beautiful there in the summer, when the white geese gather around the shore. In winter too it's like a fairytale when the snowflakes fall. But we left, together, after a simple wedding. How our mothers cried.

When I reminded Stavros after five years that we were still here in exile, Stavros said, 'The main thing is that we are together.'

'Pharmachio! (expensive like a) pharmacy!' said Dad, when Mum and I returned from our mission to lift the evil eye.

'The poor woman has to make ends meet somehow,' my mother said.

'I wish I could work cash in hand,' said Dad.

'It was worth it, Chrissie's looking better already, aren't you Darling? Now go lie down before we have dinner.'

I obeyed my mother and went to my room. It was true, I did feel a little bit better. I tried to recall exactly what Mrs Mavros had done. Her tools of trade could not have been more basic: a needle hanging from a black thread and holy water. This was regular tap water that had been infused with basil and blessed in church. 'Basilia' means *king* in Greek. On the hierarchy of herbs it stands at number one.

Mrs Mavros started by swinging the needle gently over my head. I took that to be the diagnosis part. 'Definitely the evil eye,' she said to Mum after observing its movement. Then she went on to the cure part. 'Take three small sips of water,' she instructed. Mrs Mavros mumbled some prayers as I complied, like a patient in a doctor's surgery. 'I can feel it lifting,' she said; then to my mother, 'See her eyes Voula, brighter already.' Mrs Mavros certainly had the gift of suggestion. I was reminded of the fable of the Emperor's new clothes. Still, I liked her and decided there and then that I'd go back without my mother, and ask her to read my coffee cup. For Mrs Mavros was also known for having the gift of prophecy. Was there any chance at all that things would work out between me and George? I had to know. I was so utterly miserable with unseemly love for my cousin. I needed some hope for the future. Perhaps Mrs Mavros would be able to see something worth living for, some glimmer of something good in my miserable life. Then I remembered I already had a boyfriend: James.

I got the chance to visit the widow the following Saturday evening when Mum and Dad left the house, all dressed up to go to the Greek cinema in Northcote. James wasn't due to pick me up for another hour, perfect. I was nervous as hell as I knocked on her back door. I hoped no one had seen me walk down the side of her house. Mrs

Mavros brewed up Greek coffee exactly as Mum did, in a copper *briki*. 'See the sludge at the bottom of the cup?' she said after I'd drunk my coffee. 'That's where the future is hidden. Now swirl the cup around and turn it upside down on your saucer.' Mrs Mavros saw images in the blotches of residual coffee clinging to the sides of the small cup. She put on an elegant pair of glasses and peered inside. 'I see a boy, no wait ... it's not a boy, it's a man,' she said theatrically. I put to the back of mind that most girls my age would consult her about matters of the heart. 'And I see an airplane, I see travel.' I dragged my chair closer. 'Someone is going away,' Mrs Mavros said.

'Could it mean someone is back?' I asked.

'That is entirely possible,' said the widow.

'Life in this lucky country was very, very difficult when we first came out,' my mother tells me. I wonder if she's sharing her woes as a way of encouraging me to confide in her, but I'm actually not very interested in her tales, and I've no intention of telling her about my lustful feeling for her brother's son. 'At home in my village I had a mother and three sisters, here I had no one.'

'What about Dad?' I ask, eager to contradict. 'Or Uncle Nick? He's your brother.'

'Men,' she states simply, like that explains everything.

'What about Aunt Eleni?'

'That woman is a saint. But it's not the same as a blood relation. I can't tell her things I would tell one of my sisters.' She looked into the distance, as if to find them there. 'I even miss their voices yelling at me, *Voula! Have you been to the water pump? We need to do the dishes. Quickly now.* I was the youngest girl in the family. I never learned to cook or do the laundry.' That's weird, I thought to myself, because that's all you seem to do now. 'I was a tomboy. I could run as fast as my brother and I could climb much higher in the mulberry trees, because I was as light as a squirrel. I remember yelling down to your Uncle Nikos one day, *You'll have to move faster than that if you ever want to catch yourself a wife.*'

At least I'm not as ugly as you, he said to hurt me. But I laughed, I knew I wasn't ugly. I yelled back, *One day I will have a handsome husband, lots of pretty children and a house near our mother.* She got quiet and I wonder how long I have to wait before I can go and get ready for my date with James.

I'm about to walk away when Dad picks up the story. 'As it turned out you married the handsomest man of all,' he says and they both laugh. 'You know I could have had my pick of any girl in our part of Thessaloniki. But when I went back to my parents' village to visit my *yiayia*, I caught sight of your mother,' he says. 'Men like natural women, with long hair and no make-up. Remember that when you're looking for a husband.'

'Dad! I've got a boyfriend, remember?'

'So you're serious about this Jimmy?'

'James. His name is James, Dad.'

He ignores this comment and continues with his story. 'When I said I was going to try my luck in Australia, her mother cried.' Dad looks over at Mum. 'I said, we'll be back in two or three years. We're not staying there forever, just long enough to make some money. Your mother's brother Nikos was already here and making good money working double shifts at General Motors.'

'We didn't realise that we'd end up *stuck* here,' says Mum. She says the 'stuck' in English for emphasis. I resent the negative implication, because although I've been nowhere else, I just know Melbourne is the best place in the entire world.

'The stories we heard about Australia were like fairy tales: so many jobs you could pick and choose, kangaroos hopping down the main street, and that it was always warm, no snow.'

'That part was true,' I exclaimed.

'I can't start the car some mornings it is so cold,' said Dad, 'and I have to pour hot water over the frozen windows.'

'So cold,' echoes Mum.

In our house it's always two against one.

Attraction

I cannot believe what has happened. Something wonderful and also terrifying. Me, Magdalena Mavros, the widow, the most reserved and quiet woman in the neighbourhood, having eyes for another woman's husband! Lord forgive me, but I feel happy. He came into my home two days ago with his wife. She has come to see me many times before, but until now has always come alone. 'I'm suffering,' she said to me, 'I can hardly stand straight with this headache. My husband had to help me walk over here.' The first thing I noticed was his full moustache, a sign of virility. He didn't say a word, just helped her to a chair and went to wait outside. I could barely concentrate on lifting the evil eye curse, for thinking of this woman's husband. It can't be easy for him, to live with a woman such as this. My guess is that she's hiding something, a secret that tears at her from the inside.

Then today he called by, alone. 'My wife has been singing your praises,' he said, then added that he'd noticed one of the kitchen taps was dripping. 'I came to change the washer for you,' he said. I made him coffee and he said, 'I don't believe all this mumbo jumbo with the cups.'

'Don't worry,' I said, 'no charge for this.' He smiled and we talked some more. Then when I saw him to the door he looked at me in a way that made me frightened. I sensed that he had seen me, as no one has since Stavros passed away.

So now I will wait. Perhaps I will see him around the neighbourhood, or it may be that he will come over again on some pretence as he did today.

In those long ago days before instant messaging and email, a person waited for the post and savoured every letter and card. On the tram into work I reread a postcard from George which I'd been carrying around with me the entire week. In 1982 I was twenty-two and in many ways my life was only just beginning. I'd recently got my first job, doing window displays for Myer in the city, as well as my first serious boyfriend. The picture of Santorini on George's post card looked like it had been taken decades before. The blue of the ocean was deeply saturated and contrasted dramatically with the white sugar cube-like buildings that clung to the cliff face. George started his note with some lines of poetry by Cavafy. I remembered how much I'd loved this poem too, when we did it at Greek school.

When you start on your journey to Ithaca,
Then pray that the road is long,
Full of adventure, full of knowledge.

No doubt George was having all kinds of adventures in Athens, teaching English. Meanwhile back home my Melbourne adventures involved a variety of alcoholic beverages and the challenge of getting into my room late at night without waking up Mum and Dad. At the same time I was constantly negotiating my relationship with my new boyfriend James.

'You're an adult,' James said to me, again and again, 'remind me why exactly you can't sleep over. My parents are cool with it.'

And from my parents, 'What kind of unmarried girl stays out until three in the morning? Are you promised to him in some way? Have you given *logo*, your word? Are you engaged?'

James and I met at an exhibition opening while George was away. I was close to finishing my painting degree at the time, and was impressed that James was a real artist who painted in a studio rather than his bedroom at home. I couldn't believe it when he asked for my phone number. On our first date he took me to Rumbarella's on Brunswick Street. After our meal he led me to the exhibition space upstairs, where he had two small canvases on display. Then on the way down the narrow wooden steps he let go of my hand, turned around and kissed me. I felt like the luckiest girl in the world.

We'd been going out for almost six months when I was offered the window display job at Myer. It wasn't exactly what I'd dreamed of after graduation. I'd had many a fantasy of my own solo show, where champagne flowed and the critics lined up to tell me I was the new Brett Whiteley; but it was a steady job that allowed me some creativity, and it was a lot better than most of the jobs my classmates had found – the ones who were working at all.

James accused me of selling out, which hurt. I kept my mouth shut somehow. Even if he never said so, I knew his parents were paying the rent for his studio. As it turned out I had a flair for display work and was soon promoted and had to advertise for an assistant. That was how I met, or rather was reunited with Jerry.

Jerry was named after Jerome Robbins, the choreographer. He told me he grew up to a soundtrack of Broadway musicals: *West Side Story, Cabaret, Sweet Charity* and occasionally, when things were going well for his mother, *The Pyjama Game.* He had never met his father. His mother chose all Jerry's clothes when he was little, and never let him dirty them out of doors. He was all she had and she couldn't risk anything happening to him. No one who knew them ever doubted that Jerry would grow up to be gay. He said he simply never had the option of being straight.

I remembered noticing Jerry on the first day of my final year at art school. He was one of the new first year boys. It was the early eighties and he dressed with chronological accuracy: he wore ripped jeans, a string vest over a white singlet with a red bandana around his neck. He also wore heavy black eyeliner. Jerry looked me up and down as we passed one another in the stairwell at college, almost leeringly I thought at the time. Later I realised that he was simply checking out my outfits. When we became friends at Myer, he often borrowed my clothes.

It was in the windowless staff tea room, that our paths crossed again. Queuing up for a cup of tea at the ancient urn we saw one another and laughed. Jerry was working in lady's scarves. The customers loved him, but I wrangled things so that Jerry reported directly to me. He invited me over for dinner at his place to celebrate his new role, and we talked until two in the morning. Jerry lived in a one bedroom flat in St Kilda with his dachshund, Dean Martin. On that first visit, Jerry played Judy Garland records at such a volume that I had trouble hearing our conversation. But Jerry had a terrible secret. I found out about it accidentally, many years later. In his room, behind the mirrored doors of his closet, in an orange plastic milk crate was an alternate record collection. In the evenings, when he was alone and wearing headphones, Jerry listened to Cold Chisel and AC/DC.

Desire

I saw my moustachioed man at the milk bar today. Ding went the bell on the door as I entered and thump went my heart. *Kalimera*, he said tipping his head as he left. *Kalimera*, I replied. Did he notice me catching my breath? The smell of *Brylcreem* in his hair made me swoon. My husband Stavros had also used this cream to keep his hair in place.

'What can I get for you today Mrs Mavros?' asked Maria who runs the store.

'The man who just walked out!' I wanted to say. Instead I answered in a surprisingly calm voice, 'a jar of tomato paste, please Maria, and a packet of *paximathia*.' I wondered how many times I had run into him before the other day when he visited with his wife. How many times had I walked past him here or around the neighbourhood, without seeing him.

So now even I have a secret. I've often said that love may be for the young, but luckily for me and the good living I make from reading cups, secrets are for everybody.

I fell in love with James Black on the night we met. I believe it was because of the symmetry of his features: the green of his perfect eyes, his perfectly straight nose and the centre part of his blonde hair. His background also impressed me. I said at the outset that I was superficial. James had gone to a fancy private school, one that had a boat-house on the Yarra. He rowed, which seemed terribly *Brideshead Revisited* to me. He cycled competitively, played the piano and spoke beautifully. His use of sarcasm was legendary. I thought him funny as well as handsome. I never quite understood what he saw in me. The only option I ever had for extra curricular activity was Greek school.

James and I had been a couple for almost a year before he invited me over for dinner to meet his family. It was a Friday night and they were having take-away. At the end of the evening, when I got home and told my mother, she refused to believe me. 'You mean to say you were invited for a meal and his mother didn't cook?' My mother gasped. I didn't tell her that I almost didn't eat. The 'vegetarian' pizza I had ordered was covered in shredded ham. Mrs Black was furious. She called up the local pizza place and demanded they make me another small vegetarian pan pizza, and this time without the ham. Of course, they said, it would take twenty minutes. Satisfied with her assertiveness and the calibre of her hospitality she sat down to eat; as did everyone else.

'This pizza's delicious,' exclaimed James's father.

'Lots of cheese, just the way I like it,' added James's sister.

I swallowed my saliva silently. Twenty minutes never passed more slowly. I wanted to cry but forced a smile on my face. My cheeks hurt. No one noticed. One by one they finished their meals and left the table. Mrs Black loaded the dishwasher.

'Darling,' she said to her husband. 'Chrissie's pizza will be ready now.'

'Right you are,' he said picking up his car keys. He winked at me good naturedly, 'back soon.'

Don't cry, don't cry, don't cry. A crust of bread, some peanuts, a tic tac: nothing was offered to me. Ten minutes later Mr Black was back. It had been almost an hour since the initial phone order. I ate alone at the table. James didn't want to miss *Dallas* on telly. What upset me most was that I was not given the chance to explain that I'm not a vegetarian. I would have happily eaten the original pizza.

You wouldn't think you'd have a future with someone like that, from a family like that. And yet we were already making plans to move in together.

'So, when do I get to meet James?' George asked. 'Tina's told me all about him. She said he's dreamy.' He clasped his hands over his heart and smiled.

'Yeah, we should all get together sometime,' I said vaguely.

'When Dora arrives we can go out as a foursome,' said George.

'Great.'

'But until then, let's get a group together, otherwise I'll feel like the third wheel tagging along with you and him.' Or else James will, I thought.

And so we found ourselves at one of the city's independent cinemas on a Saturday night, watching an Iranian film about war and rape. It had been James's choice. Afterwards we went for drinks.

'Hi guys,' said the waiter, 'table for six?'

We sat outdoors watching the theatre crowd from next door disperse. A tram rattled past and George said, 'This is all so Melbourne.' He had the most beautiful smile.

'Did you ever think about staying in Greece,' asked my friend Jerry, 'rather than bringing Dora to live out here?'

'We talked about that a lot,' George said swirling his red wine and taking a sip. His lips were so full, spongy to kiss I imagined. 'But she was quite keen to leave and to travel. She's never been outside of Greece,' George said.

'Is that right?' said James, scowling.

'Most of the people over there that I met have never travelled abroad,' said George. 'They all take their holidays in Greece.'

'I suppose they have all those islands,' said Jerry, 'and all that sunshine, why go any place else?'

'Narrow lives,' said James. And I realised quite suddenly that James looked his most handsome when straight faced and serious, as he was now.

'You're very quiet,' George said, touching my arm. James gave us a look. Or was it just my guilt.

'Well I'm off,' said Jerry gulping down what was left of his champagne. 'There's a man in a dance club somewhere out there who has my name on him. Or will do as soon as I can get him to a tattooist!' He stood up and gave me a quick peck on the cheek. 'I'll see you at work on Monday, Sweets.'

'Call me tomorrow,' I said, 'if there's anything to report.'

'Bye all. Nice to have finally met you,' he said to George; and with a woosh of his scarf, Jerry disappeared. I did hope that Jerry would meet someone tonight, someone he could have a real relationship with. As far as I knew he'd been going from one one-night stand to another for years, and not because he wanted to. He was simply still waiting for Mr Right.

I was lost in thought and for a while we were all quiet. I finished my wine. George and James both ordered espresso. Tina and her friend Katy, who had recently gone back to using her Greek name,

Kanella, decided on hot chocolate.

'He's cute,' Kanella said, to no one in particular.

'Too bad he's gay,' said Tina.

'Always the way,' her friend added.

'I don't understand why women always say that,' James said tersely. 'There are plenty of good looking straight men around. Sometimes I think women are simply attracted to the unattainable.'

'I agree with you James,' said George. 'That's one thing I like about Greek women, the ones in Greece I mean,' he said, excluding Tina, Kanella and me dismissively. 'They're very upfront and know exactly what they want. You wouldn't catch any of them mooning over a gay guy.'

'Well good for them,' I said, catching the waiter's eye. 'We'll have the bill thanks.'

Lust

Today my moustachioed man brought me *melomakarona,* a honey soaked Greek biscuit. 'Whenever Eleni makes these it's like she's feeding the entire Greek army,' he said off handedly. I noticed that they were on a paper plate.

'I can't take them,' I said.

'Please don't be offended. I just …' he paused looking very uncomfortable. 'You see I have to watch my sugar levels and my wife always makes far too many.'

I didn't like it when he said 'my wife' and I suddenly felt jealous. I know it's ridiculous but don't all matters of the heart have something of the ridiculous about them? He continued, 'I thought since you live alone you probably don't bake for the masses as some of the ladies of this neighbourhood do.'

'I'm allergic to honey,' I said. He looked both relieved and confused.

'Excuse me, I don't wish to question you, but I've never heard of such a thing. A Greek, allergic to honey? It's like an Italian who won't eat spaghetti.'

I laughed. 'A coffee while you're here?' I turned towards the cupboard to get the coffee jar. It was then he touched me for the first time. He put his hands on my shoulders and turned me around. As he spoke he looked into my eyes like he was reaching into my very core.

'Beautiful Magdalena. Do you know, I think you have bewitched me,' he said. The colour came to my face and I felt both hot and uncomfortable, and yet completely happy. 'Can I come to see you again?' he asked, 'Perhaps one evening? I can slip out of the house unnoticed sometimes.'

'I don't think that's a good idea,' I forced myself to say.

'I don't either,' he said, letting me go. It was like the flame in my chest that kept me alive was drenched in water. A million disappointments condensed into a dark lump inside of me. 'It's a terrible idea, but I think I will go mad if I don't hold you against me, even once,' he said. And then he kissed me.

Mrs Evans had lived across the road from our family for as long as I could remember. With no guidelines or training, she instinctively did what *Neighbourhood Watch* formalised, decades later. Mum and Dad liked the fact that Mrs Evans kept an eye out over the street; but they found it peculiar that in all the years of being neighbours she had never once invited them inside her home. All their conversations were over the front fence. They had asked her in many times, but she always said she didn't want to intrude. Even at Christmas when Mrs Evans made coconut ice for all the neighbours, she knocked on our front door and passed the paper plate across the doorway, a threshold she seemed unable to cross. My mother and all our Greek neighbours never used disposable plates. Whenever anyone brought sweets over, their plate was always returned with a different cake or biscuit on it. It was considered rude to return an empty plate. Gladys Evans never gave my mother the chance to return a plate with some of her baked goods on it, perhaps a sweet pumpkin *pita* or a 'hairy' vermicelli covered *kataifi*.

Gladys Evans lived alone, except for Trudi the terrier. Dog years to human years they were like twin sisters. Mrs Evans's husband had died years earlier and her three sons had all moved out of home. The only one I remembered was the youngest, Trevor, who was the same age as George and who we called Trevor the skip. There had been a time when we all played together, Trevor and George, the spaghetti brothers, Val and Kanella, Val's brother Nick, and his best friend Nick the wog. The entire street was our playground from morning until night. We played footy in the winter, cricket in summer and chasey, hopscotch and hide and seek all year round. It was during a game of hidey that I saw Mrs Evans throw away a plate of *moussaka* that my mother had dropped off earlier that day. I recalled how much care Mum had put into making the *moussaka* and the way she carefully wrapped a large portion to take over to 'that poor old lady'.

I was hiding behind a clump of hydrangeas, and feeling a little guilty for venturing to the side of Trevor's place. Normally we only hid in front gardens up and down the street. I wondered whether I'd gone too far and would never be found. I imagined myself emerging at night, like a possum and being reprimanded by George and the others. It was from this secret spot that I saw Mrs Evans empty my mother's plate of food into Trudi's bowl. The dog sniffed tentatively at the potato and eggplant dish, then turned her nose up in imitation of her mistress.

'Don't blame you Trudi Love,' said the old woman, picking up the dog bowl and tapping out its contents onto a sheet of newspaper. Mrs Evans bent low, wrapped the whole thing up and put it into her metal bin, letting out a few groans as she did so. A few minutes later she came out with a can of dog food for Trudi and a cup of tea and some raisin toast for herself. 'Far too oily, their food is, isn't it Trudi my dear?' A blob of butter clung to her bristly upper lip.

'Chrissie!' screamed Trevor. 'Found ya.' He ran back out to the street and I followed, very glad to be out of there. From the corner of my eye I saw Mrs Evans shaking her head disapprovingly. The dog seemed to be doing the same.

Intimacy

So now we have become intimate, my moustachioed man and me. What pleasure to be held by someone strong and full of life. It's life I miss. If only I'd known how little time I'd have with Stavros, we might have hurried along and had some children. Nothing fills a home like a child, my mother always said.

A merry widow, the Aussies might call me. But there is nothing merry about being widowed at twenty-nine. *Why are you marrying an old man?* my mother had asked. My father responded for me, *He's only twelve years older, that is as it should be*. What about Stavros getting lung cancer, was that also as it should be?

'You're beautiful,' my moustachioed man said to me, 'and you're all mine because everyone else is blind.' And yet I was the one who sought invisibility. Hiding behind my black clothing. But to be truly seen, by someone as virile as him, is glorious.

Above the bed I shared with Stavros is a large black and white photograph taken after our wedding at a photographer's studio. I wore a hired dress that many brides had worn before me. Stavros wore his one good suit. I knew I could not make love under that photograph, so I lead my soon-to-be lover to the back bedroom. I was extremely nervous. The only man I had ever been with, in that way, was my husband. I drew the blinds and shut the door, and with it the outside world. For the time we had together I was not the widow, not the foreigner, not the reader of cups and the lifter of curses. I was just Magdalena.

Then after he left I lay there with my long hair loose, feeling happier than I had been for so many years. I put my face to his pillow and breathed in his masculine scent. It made my stomach flutter. Heavens, I'm like a schoolgirl again.

The police report stated 'no sign of forced entry.' It was an inside job, no doubt about it. When my parents returned home after a long visit with my mother's cousin Soula, they immediately noticed that things were missing. The stereo from the living room was gone, although the television remained. All the records were taken. From the kitchen, at first it seemed everything was intact, although later after the police had gone, when my father went to make a sandwich, he discovered the bread knife was nowhere to be found. The young police officer filled in his paper work with a calmness swaddled in boredom. He saw this sort of thing every day, often many times a day.

'Aren't you going to dust for fingerprints?' my mother asked. She was a big fan of *Homicide* and *Division 4*. He didn't even pretend to listen.

'Anything gone from the bedrooms?'

'Our room is untouched,' said my mother. 'But they've taken almost everything from my daughter's room.'

'Can I see?' They walked back up the passageway and into my bare room. I'd left the posters on the walls. They were out of date anyway. I no longer listened to The Police or The Sex Pistols. 'Your daughter seems to have moved out of home and neglected to tell you,' the policeman said.

When I'd broached the subject of moving out of home a couple of weeks beforehand, my mother had closed the conversation with a sharp, 'Don't ever speak to me about this! You can move out of home when you're married.' I took her at her word and organised the move without another word. We collected boxes from the local supermarket and borrowed James's mate Robo's ute.

I took the bread knife because it reminded me of Dad. Slicing the bread was a man's job in our house. Most days he drew the thin serrated blade through heavy loaves of pasta durra, to make sweet sandwiches with store bought *halva*, to take to the barber shop for lunch. And I started to make them for myself, after leaving my parent's home.

James found us a small single storey terrace in Prahran to rent. It was close to the studio he shared with a couple of our friends from art school. As a bonus, James said, our landlord lived next door. If anything needed attending to, we only had to knock.

We were now living on the other side of the river from my parents, but it was as if the Greek chorus had followed us. The landlord's wife, Mrs Xanthos was none other than the sister of Mrs Mavros, the widow. Her husband wasn't dead, but he may as well have been, for all the attention she gave him. The woman was much more interested in me, the Greek girl who had moved out of her parents' home before getting married … and with an Australian!

In some ways it was worse than living at home. Mrs Xanthos was nosier than my mother, and I saw her just about every day; either in the morning as I headed off for work, or at the other end of the day as I arrived home. She was almost always in the front garden keeping an eye out over the street, rather like Mrs Evans. No one could accuse her of neglecting the plants out the front of her home, and I never saw a front stoop swept clean so regularly. I wondered if the back garden got as much attention.

Mrs Xanthos was nice enough. She smiled and said *kalimera*, good morning, but in her eyes I detected confusion. I was polite, I spoke very good Greek and yet I was clearly a slut.

Gossip

I had the most unexpected visit today, from the Australian lady who lives down the road, Mrs Evans. I've seen her walking to High Street and back with her buggy and that small dog of hers. The beast reminds me of the ferrets that were used in my town to make fur coats. Not that I would ever tell Mrs Evans that; the dog is her closest companion, despite having three sons with wives and eight grandchildren. It appears having children is no insurance against loneliness. When I answered her vigorous knocking she said, 'I hear you read coffee cups, Dearie.' Mercifully she'd left her dog at home. 'Yes,' I said, and invited her in. 'Your English is very good,' she said a short time later. Like we're all illiterate. The town I grew up in was prosperous; we had a large population of Jews before the war, cultured people. I did French at school and Latin. I wanted to ask her how many languages she spoke.

Anyway, it turns out she didn't come to me to ask, but to tell. She was bursting with news, about Chrissie. How did she know I'd be interested? Mrs Evans said, 'I keep an eye out over the street.' Tell me something I didn't know, I wanted to say. 'Chrissie has moved out with her boyfriend, you may have seen him, tall and very good looking, but uppity,' she lifted her nose in the air. I nodded in agreement. 'You know who else is very good looking,' she said at the door before leaving, 'Chrissie's Uncle, Mr Nikos. And such a friendly man too.' I froze, but tried to remain calm.

'Perhaps next time I will read your cup Mrs Evans,' I said.

'Cheery-bye,' she replied, leaving me with a disconcerting wink.

It was Sunday and I was at a loose end. When I called Mum to give her my new address and phone number, and invite her and Dad over to see the house, she said, 'We'll visit you when you're married.' Then before I could say anything else, she cut me off with, 'I have to finish the mopping now Chrissie, good-bye.' Of course, it was Sunday. I couldn't help but think back to the regularity of Sundays at home when I was little, with Dad at the *kafenio* and Mum and I cleaning. It all seemed a lifetime ago. What to do now? James was at his studio, calling George was out of the question, as was calling Jerry who never emerged until the pm on Sundays. After checking what was on telly, nothing of course, it occurred to me to try Tina. Sure we'd never been close, not like George and I, but from time to time we did do some cousin to cousin bonding.

On the steps of Flinders Street Station, under the clocks, Tina and I stopped to check out some surfie looking boys from another high school. When they looked over at us we just giggled and walked away. It was correction day 1974 or perhaps 1975 and we were buzzing with our first taste of independence and the thrill of a day off school. We arrived in the city dressed almost identically in high waisted flared jeans, which hovered over dangerously high cork sole shoes, like space ships waiting to abduct unsuspecting human beings. We paired these with teeny tiny short sleeve cardigans. Our eye shadow was blue, our lips glossy pink, and our biggest wish in life was to be *Dolly* magazine cover girls.

'Which film do you want to see?' I asked Tina.

'I thought we were going shopping,' she said. 'I'm dying to go into *The House of Merrivale and Mr John*. I've always been too scared to go in on my own, the sales girls are so beautiful.'

'I'll go with you,' I said, 'but they're replaying an old *Monty Python* film and I'd really like to see it.'

'OK,' said Tina, 'first we'll do a little shopping, and then we'll go to see your film.'

She was right about the sales girls, it was almost impossible to differentiate them from the mannequins. Both had perfect smooth skin, and were devoid of all expression. The shop itself was dimly lit, and every piece of clothing as well as every counter was covered in feathers, sequins or glittery scarves. It was excruciatingly glamorous, and despite the big effort Tina and I had both made with our appearance, we felt daggy and out of place. It was a relief to get to Hoyts on Bourke Street. The black and orange foyer was also cool but unintimidating, and it was full of kids our own age. It put us instantly in the mood for a box of jaffas to go with our Smiths Crisps and small tubs of vanilla ice-cream. In the queue for these treats we ran into George and Trevor.

'I am *not* sitting with my brother,' said Tina.

'I'll sit next to him,' I said, 'then you can sit next to me.'

'And now for something completely different,' the film began with an animated foot coming down upon the opening title. It was silliness from beginning to end, and I laughed so much I thought I might throw up my jaffas.

'There's just one thing I don't get,' said Tina, as we stepped outside into the sunlight. 'Which one was Monty Python?'

Trevor, George and I glanced at one another and started laughing.

'What's so funny? Was he the tall one with the moustache?'

It was impossible to answer.

Tina's voice got louder, 'Stop laughing! What's so funny? I don't get it.' I gasped for breath, my stomach hurt more than it had watching the film. And the more Tina got annoyed, the funnier it seemed to be. I wasn't trying to be mean, I just couldn't stop.

'You two always gang up on me,' Tina said. 'I don't know why you came into the city with me Chrissie, you obviously just want to hang out with George, like you always do.'

Tina shook her head before speaking, like a lion accentuating its mane. Her honey blonde hair had been permed since the last time I'd seen her and was bigger than ever. My hair was dark brown, like George's, and short. Tina and I looked like members of different tribes rather than cousins.

'How's James?' Tina asked after we'd ordered our coffees.

'He's well. Working hard on his paintings for the show later this year. God knows what I'm doing with my life.'

'Seems to me you're doing great,' she said. I gave Tina a quizzical look. 'You've got a gorgeous boyfriend, you've moved out of home, which I am so jealous of, and you've got a great job. What else do you want?'

'I don't know. I just kind of wish I was doing something more creative with my life. I feel flat,' I said, glancing at her hair. The waiter brought our drinks and winked at Tina, ignoring me completely. She didn't seem to notice.

'I know what you mean. I keep comparing myself to George. He's so full of energy these days, getting his *Nectar* project off the ground,' Tina said.

'So he's told you about it?'

'Have you ever known George to keep a secret?' We laughed. 'Between bouts of moaning about how he misses Dora, he's super productive: teaching, planning the wedding and all the *Nectar of the Gods* business. I don't know how he does it.'

'That's George though, isn't it? Always upbeat,' I said taking another sip of coffee.

'I really shouldn't compare myself to him,' Tina said. 'I've always hated it when other people do it.' I nodded. 'George is the friendly one, Tina is the quiet one,' she said. 'You don't know how lucky you are being an only child.'

'Doesn't feel like it, sometimes,' I said.

'I overheard Mum and Dad telling some friends of theirs that I was aloof! I mean if your own parents don't realise you're shy, rather than stuck up, what hope have you got with strangers?'

'You must have misunderstood them,' I said, finishing my coffee. We were quiet for a few moments. I looked around for the waiter; he'd forgotten to bring us glasses of water. I spotted him at the counter chatting up another girl.

'Greek men are such womanisers aren't they?' I said.

'Ninety-nine percent of them,' said Tina.

'You seeing anyone?' I asked.

'There is someone actually,' Tina said coyly.

'Not Greek?' I ventured.

'No. But it's early days. It'll probably go nowhere. Like all my other relationships.'

'Can I get you another coffee *koukla*?' the waiter said, suddenly appearing and smiling at Tina.

'I'm fine.' Tina said without looking at him.

'Can I have a glass of water?' I said, as he walked away.

'You and George seem to have drifted, since he got back from Greece,' Tina said suddenly, changing the subject.

'Well it's all Dora this and Dora that these days,' I replied without thinking.

'You sound a bit jealous,' Tina said. I looked at her blankly. 'Just stirring Chrissie! Gee you've gone white. I'm only teasing.'

'I know,' I said, taking a last sip of water. 'Shall we get the bill?'

Tina nodded and I tried my best to smile. I couldn't get away from thinking about George. What on earth was I to do about him? As I stood to leave, I took a passing look into my empty coffee cup, hoping for a clue; but my future seemed drained of meaning.

Trust

So now it has been three times, and each time has been wonderful and world stopping. I am only saying the truth, it's like my life stops when he is with me, like we are in another place where nothing else matters. I've lost my appetite and two kilos already. I should be careful because I know people will talk. Gossip spreads quickly, passed along like colds in winter. Not only up and down our street, but throughout the neighbourhood and across the Yarra and back again. If I'm not careful even my sister Panayiota in Prahran will hear of it. I know how eagerly other people's secrets are shared in my line of work.

Even he has started to talk, to tell me things about his family. He speaks of his saintly wife who has stopped being a wife in the bedroom and his fair haired daughter, 'Beautiful as Aphrodite,' he says. And he bemoans his headstrong son who disappeared for several years and has now come home engaged.

'Plenty of Greek girls here in Australia, here in Melbourne and he wants someone from the old country. They're different from us Magdalena,' he said to me. 'The ones who've stayed behind, they don't have our sense of adventure, our thirst for a better life.'

Such a good father, my Nikos. Yes I will call him mine, for the time being at least.

When I told James that my friend Jerry had four audience tickets for *Countdown*. He said, 'You're a bit old for that, aren't you?' In 1985, in the circles James and I mixed in, *Countdown* was derided as being totally uncool, and yet I never missed it.

'It'll be fab,' I replied. Not that I particularly cared if he came or not. I had invited Tina to come with me, and I knew it would be more fun without James. His cynical streak often spoiled my silliness. It was Aunt Eleni who suggested that George take the spare ticket, when Jerry's friend Matt came down with the flu.

'Moping around the house won't help time move any faster,' she said to him. 'Forget Dora for a day and go out and have some fun.' I wished he'd forget about her forever. I had to constantly remind myself that romance with George was never going to happen, that it was wrong and our parents would have triple heart attacks. It had taken my mother over a month to acknowledge my move out of home and even now she and Dad rarely called and still hadn't visited. Did I really want to bring more shame to our family? And yet every night as I lay next to James, I fantasized about George. In my crazy scenarios he was obsessed with me and couldn't live without me. Of course I loved James too, but what do they say about forbidden fruit tasting sweeter? Perhaps that's all it was. I'd get over George eventually. I had to; he was getting married in six weeks. Dora's residency papers had finally come through, a date for the wedding was set and the church had been booked.

'I bet I'll be the oldest one here,' George mumbled as we were led inside the television studio. 'How did I let Mum talk me into this?' The audience was mostly made up of teenage girls, many with hair that rivalled Tina's in volume. As if reading my mind, Tina pulled out a blue, wide pronged comb from her enormous bag, and ran it through her hair before the show started. 'I hope I don't run into any of my students,' George said. He was teaching in a Catholic girls school by day until *Nectar of the Gods* started making money. I'd seen him on a number of mornings as we both left for work, when I still lived at home, and recalled how straight and yet sexy he looked in a shirt and tie. This afternoon he was in his usual Levis and black t-shirt: simple, timeless and incredibly hot! Stop it, I told myself, he's your first cousin and he's engaged to someone else.

The show began with a live act. Jerry, Tina and I quickly got caught up in the excitement; we cheered, clapped and danced with the rest of the teens. And before long, George joined in too.

'Admit it,' I said, 'you're having fun.' He just smiled. It made my heart race. The day was turning out better than I had imagined. I was especially enjoying rubbing up against George as we danced. The slight dampness of his t-shirt against my bare arm gave me goose bumps. Not for the first time I wondered how my feelings for him could feel so right when they were clearly wrong.

Halfway through the show the stage manager directed us to the other side of the studio. A second stage had been set up there for a new band called Photon. 'Science Nerds,' George said. Never the less when they came on stage I noticed that the lead singer was really cute. So cute that I couldn't take my eyes away from him. George yelled in my ear, above the music, 'Does the earring in his left ear mean he's gay?' I shrugged and kept my eyes on singing Science Boy. After the song he crouched down to sign autographs for the audience.

'Who's got some paper?' I frantically asked. Tina reached into her carry-all and came out with some lined notebook paper.

'What are you doing?' George asked.

'I'm getting his autograph, he's a spunk.'

'His eyes are a bit too close together,' George said.

I held up my piece of paper, trying to get the singer's attention.

'Just a couple more,' said the stage manager to the crowd. 'The boys have to get going.'

'Please, me!' I called out, and Science Boy looked straight at me.

'What's your name?' he asked.

'Chrissie,' I said and spelled it out. When he handed back my piece of paper, I deciphered, *Please me Chrissie, love Roger.*

'I'm going to sleep with this under my pillow,' I said half jokingly.

'What a bloody waste of time,' said George, as they marched us out of the studio.

I was going back to my old street for the first time since moving in with James, for Uncle Nick's annual name day party. James had other plans, so I was going alone. Perhaps tonight would be the right time to say something to George. I remembered how jealous my cousin seemed to get at *Countdown*, and wondered if it were possible that he had inappropriate feelings towards me too. Dora was due to arrive from Greece in only a couple of weeks. My time for winning George over was quickly disappearing, like sugar melting into water.

I did everything I could think of to make myself irresistible. I bought a new dress, shaved my legs and curled my eyelashes. I wore pink lipstick and spent ages on my make-up. I also decided to make *galaktoboureko*, George's favourite dessert, to take with me. I had only recently begun to cook. There had been no need before moving in with James, and Mum had never trusted me in the kitchen after the gas incident. I read and reread every line of the recipe I found in *The Mediterranean Cookbook*, a 21st present that I'd never used. I would follow it to the letter, for I had no sense of these things called flavours. I had eaten this vanilla slice-like dessert many times. I knew how it should look, and I'd always liked the textures of the paperish filo pastry and the creamy filling. 'Gala' means *milk* in Greek.

I measured out all the ingredients carefully. What I lacked in intuition I would make up for with accuracy. Firstly I made the syrup, measuring sugar and water with chemistry class precision, then while that cooled I began work on the custard-like filling. I knew this would be the trickiest part. I heated the milk and infused it with fresh lemon peel and a sprinkling of vanilla powder. I worked quickly with the ready made filo pastry, as instructed, so that it wouldn't dry out. Back to the milk, I whisked in some flour paste to thicken, added sugar then eggs and butter. I put together the layers: filo, custard, filo, carefully yet efficiently, then popped the tray into the oven.

After forty minutes, as indicated by the recipe, I opened the oven door. It looked perfect, golden brown with small leaves of filo lifting up suggestively at the sides, begging to be eaten. I placed the tray on the sink and poured the cool syrup over the top, as evenly as I could. After a little while I put it in the fridge. The recipe had said to leave it sit overnight, but I hadn't been quite organised enough to do that, and hoped a few hours would be sufficient.

Just before leaving the house I pulled the *galaktoboureko* out of the fridge and cut it diagonally in the tray, as I'd seen done in the Greek pastry shop windows along Chapel Street. The tray resembled a patterned quilt. In the centre of each diamond I put a single fragrant clove. If presentation counted for anything I knew I'd got full marks. But how would it taste? I was suddenly gripped with anxiety. What was I trying to prove with this half baked idea? Would a blind girl seduce her lover with a painting? Would a deaf person write a song? I was clearly one egg short of a dozen, as my mother had always suspected.

With dinner finished, a scurry of small Greek women replaced all the savoury serving plates with a smorgasbord of dessert options. As well as my *galaktoboureko* there were all the traditional favourites: *kourapiethes*, crescent shaped shortbread dusted with icing sugar; baklava, layered filo pastry with walnut filling, and my aunt Eleni's *melomakarona*. Coaxed by their wives, the men gathered around first, to choose. My dad helped himself to a piece of my *galaktoboureko* and gave me a wink. I could hardly breathe with anticipation. Next it was the women and children's turn. George helped himself to one of everything. I so hoped he'd like the dessert I made. Perhaps he would be able to taste the love that I'd laced into it, just for him. I sat next to him on the couch, watching him bite into a piece. My heart pounded, I was going to say something, flirt a little, touch his arm or hold his gaze in a provocative manner. I had to do something tonight, it was my last chance before his fiancé arrived from Greece. Just as I was about to open my mouth to speak, Uncle Nick came back into the room.

'This *galaktoboureko* is incredible.' In his haste he hadn't noticed a blob of custard clinging to the tip of his moustache. 'Just like our mother used to make, Voula,' he said to Mum. She couldn't have looked more surprised if her mother had risen from the grave and joined the party. 'Is it true that you made this Chrissie?' I nodded.

'A fine cook,' said Aunt Eleni. 'But I mustn't jinx you. I sometimes accidentally give the evil eye. Twho, twho, twho.' She spat three times. This was the traditional way of deflecting an unintended curse.

'Thanks Aunty,' I said.

George nudged me. 'You're going to make someone a lovely wife,' he said. So we were back to this: childhood taunts. At that moment it was painfully clear that to George I would always be little cousin Chrissie. And I knew for certain that I was indeed cursed— cursed never to be with the man I loved. Any hope of romance had disappeared faster than the sweets on Uncle Nick's plate.

Tragedy

'*Chronia polla*, (may you live for) many years, for your name day,' I said to Nikos kissing him fully on the lips.

'It was quite a celebration,' he tells me, brushing my cheek with his strong hand.

'Was there dancing?' I asked.

'Yes, but nothing too crazy.' I smiled. 'If only you could have seen me in my youth Magdalena,' Nikos said. 'When my friend Yanni and I danced the *Tsamiko*, the girls in our village went crazy … and their mothers too!'

'Did your friend stay in Greece?' I asked.

'No, we came out to Australia together, he and Eleni and I.'

'What happened *Agape mou*, my love?' I asked, taking his hands.

'Magdalena, it's too sad a story for today,' Nikos said. But I insisted, gently. I wanted to know everything about this man who had changed my life. And so he told me. 'Yanni and Eleni had been in love since we were all in school together, and I had always been a little bit in love with both of them,' he smiled. 'I was the third wheel, as they say, but Yanni and Eleni, they didn't make me feel this way. We were as tight as thieves. Together the three of us decided to try our fortune in Australia. But with all the fuss involved with emigrating there hadn't been time for Yanni and Eleni to have a wedding, though the families had long since given *logo*, a pledge of marriage. They said, 'It doesn't matter, we'll get married in Australia and then we'll find a beautiful girl for you too Nikos.' We had it so well planned out, the three of us,' Nikos said. 'You will be our *koumbaro*, the best man at our wedding, and you will christen our first child, as tradition dictates. Then we will be family, Yanni and Eleni said.' Nikos sat down and pulled his hand through his hair. 'But when our ship docked in Ceylon, we came across some fighting in the port, in Colombo. Yanni and I stepped in to stop some men who were about to kill a beggar. I still remember it clearly. One of the men struck out and hit Yanni on the side of the head, before they ran away, the cowards.' Nikos stopped and sat silently, as did I. 'The ship's doctor said it was the position of the blow rather than its severity that caused Yanni's brain to bleed. We buried him at sea.'

A couple of weeks after Uncle Nick's name day party my mother called, a rare event that always put me on guard. I knew something was up the moment I heard the joyous tone in her voice. Nothing good could come of this. 'Dora has arrived!' she said. Like the release of *Beyond Thunderdome*, episode three of the Mad Max movie series, the anticipation had been building. Aunt Eleni had been raving about Dora for what seemed like forever. 'Her full name is Theodora,' she had said, 'You know it means a *gift from God*, in Greek. I know she will live up to her name. She has already been a gift to George.'

My mother too had signed up for the fan club. 'Better to marry early, get settled, have some children. I don't understand why young people wait so long these days. What are they waiting for? No, George has always been sensible. He'll be a wonderful husband and a terrific father. And Dora is so pretty.' She stopped to spit three times in quick succession, 'Twho, twho, twho. I don't want to jinx her.' The more excited she got, the more depressed I felt. I didn't know what to expect, but when I finally met the gift herself, I quickly decided I wanted a refund. She wasn't even that pretty, just thin and well groomed. And could it be true? Yes, no doubt about it, a mole on her left cheek. People who call them beauty spots are surely delusional.

'Dora, this is Chrissie,' George said when I visited, a week before the wedding.

'The famous Chrissie,' she said taking my hand. Her English was good. Apparently she'd been studying the language since primary school. But her accent reminded me of my mother and Aunt Eleni. She was an immigrant, like them, not like George and me.

'Nice to meet you,' I said.

'How do you know this? We just met,' she said. 'You might find you do not like me at all.' She had the same blunt manner of my parents' generation *and* the gift of prophecy. I wanted to suggest that she ditch *Nectar of the Gods* and go into business with Mrs Mavros.

'That's what we say here in Australia,' George said, looking at her adoringly. And to me, without so much as a glance, he added, 'Isn't she cute, the way she expresses herself?'

James bore the brunt of my foul mood that night. A throw away comment about out of date cream in the fridge led to an exchange of gripes that until then had been smothered. They now escaped into the air and exploded like flames finding oxygen.

'I know you can't smell the cream when it's off, but didn't you see the mould growing?'

'Give me a break James.'

'Why are you so grumpy?'

'Why are *you* so grumpy?'

'I'm grumpy because I haven't had sex for three weeks.'

'I'm tired because you never help around the house.'

'Pardon me, but I have a show on at the end of this year!'

'Does that mean I have to wash every single dish and spoon that's used in this house until then?'

'I think you're deliberately starting arguments, Chrissie.'

'Why would I do that?'

'I don't know. Have you met someone else?'

'Don't be ridiculous!' I yelled, storming off to our bedroom at the front of the house. It was then I remembered that I'd left the front door open, hoping for a movement of air through our stuffy and narrow terrace house. As I closed the door I overheard Mrs Xanthos on the telephone and realised that her front door was also open to the breeze. We had an ancient dusty screen door to protect us from thieves and mosquitoes, but there were other creatures lurking who were not so easily deflected. Mrs Xanthos would have heard everything. I slammed the front door and went to bed.

Stealth

It seems truly unbelievable that my sister and I come forth from the same womb. I keep everything to myself, and she, nothing. She speaks every thought that comes into her head. Tonight she called me, after ten o'clock to talk about the tenants next door, Nikos's niece Chrissie and her boyfriend. 'So much arguing,' she tells me. 'Doors slamming at all hours. I hate to think of how big the cracks in the walls will be.' Then she says, 'Tell me about Chrissie's family.' There is no subtlety with my sister.

'What on earth do you want to know?' I asked, 'they're a perfectly nice family.'

'Has the mother ever come to you? To have her coffee cup read? What has she done to throw her daughter into the arms of an Australian?'

'Panayiota,' I said to her, 'you know I don't discuss these things. I guard my client's personal matters.' She got off the telephone in a huff. Tomorrow I will have to call and make amends. She is my only blood relative in Australia. I could have made her so happy too. Told her that no, the mother rarely comes to me, but the daughter, Chrissie herself has been a regular visitor ever since the time Voula brought her in for the evil eye. Her lovesickness is worse than ever. I haven't quite worked out who it is yet, but it's not the Australian boyfriend. There wouldn't be any call for me and my coffee cups if it were.

I am surface girl. I sit smiling at my cousin George's wedding. Next to me is my handsome live-in boyfriend. We are the perfect couple. Even my mother thinks we look good together, and she's been against non-Greek friends and boyfriends for as long as I can remember. But underneath the smooth veneer, my mood is chipboard ugly. And so I drink. I don't know how else to endure the festivities. I'd had eight months to tell George how I felt about him. Between our ride home from the airport and his journey back there, to pick up his intended bride. But in all that time, no moment seemed right, and so I sit here now with my perfect smile, and my imperfect heart, trying to pass for happy.

George and Dora had a backyard reception. All of Uncle Nick's name day parties were like dress rehearsals for this epic event. Trestle tables circled the backyard and in the centre was a large wooden dance floor. Coloured lights were strung between trees and there was enough food and drink for twice the number of invited guests. My contribution was a cold risotto salad.

I boiled several fresh beetroot until tender, then peeled and diced the flesh. I added this to a mound of rice that had been cooked in the reserved water, staining each grain a deep crimson. To contrast, I mixed in a vibrant selection of green herbs and crushed pistachio nuts. And lastly I poured in a fiery dressing, made with sea salt, olive oil, lemon juice and a spoonful of very hot mustard. I like to put symbolism into my food, just as I used to do with my paintings at art school. The red represented blood and pain, the green represented envy and the overall hot spiciness was how I felt about my cousin George. The dish was an in-joke between me and myself. I knew I had no right to be jealous, I was living with James. But there is a chasm of difference between what is known rationally in the brain and what is felt, irrationally in the heart.

I watched Uncle Nick filling up people's glasses; he was hell bent on mass drunken revelry: singing, frenetic dancing and if all went well, some plate throwing. During his speech my uncle told the guests how beautiful the bride was and what a splendid wife she would make. 'Drink, drink!' he implored everyone at the end of his speech: and I did. In contrast to dry eyed Uncle Nick, Aunt Eleni was silent, weeping with happiness into her embroidered handkerchief.

When George rose to speak, I felt like I would never be happy again. He looked so handsome in his pinstripe suit. First he spoke in Greek and then in English. He was eloquent in both languages. His cheeks were flushed and he looked deliriously happy. What you see is what you get with George, that's one thing I love about him, his genuiness. He has none of my duplicity. When the dancing started, I decided to move on to ouzo.

'Steady on,' said James.

I had missed my chance with George, although of course we never stood a chance to begin with. We were first cousins; that was all our relationship could ever be. But that unassailable fact did not temper my dramatic gesture when, through no planning of my own, I found myself alone with him later that evening. The scene of my romantic assault was out front of the two portaloos that had been set up at the very back of the garden. I was waiting desperately to pee when George came out of one.

'All yours,' he said, holding the door open for me.

'I wish *you* were all mine,' I said, lunging at him. I stood on tip toes and draped my arms over his broad shoulders. I stared into his beautiful eyes and said what I had been thinking for so long, 'I love you George.'

'Chrissie, you're drunk,' George said, smiling nervously and disentangling my arms from around his neck. It was then that the door of the second portaloo opened and Mrs Mavros the widow came out. She walked past us without a word.

The day after George's wedding I awoke with a massive hangover. Luckily James had gone to his studio early in the day and I had the house to myself. I felt painfully embarrassed every time I thought of my declaration of love the night before, and the look on George's face. I was the last person on earth, apart from his sister, that he thought of 'in that way'. I was a complete fool. I picked up a book to read but couldn't concentrate. I felt awful, physically and mentally, and craved something warm and comforting.

I found the recipe for *avgolemono* in my trusty Mediterranean Cookbook. I had childhood memories of how it used to taste: of my mother's love and concern and of my father's kisses. The name itself means 'egg and lemon', but these ingredients are added at the end of the cooking process, to finish off the soup. The main ingredient, chicken, goes unmentioned, just as many things of significance are left unsaid.

I didn't use real chicken anyway. I was not in the mood to torment another living creature. I bought chicken stock from the supermarket and warmed it up on the stove in a saucepan. I had to buy rice too, because I didn't have the right sort. Who knew there were so many different varieties? Short-grain, Italian, jasmine, basmati, but as soon as I saw the long-grain, I knew that was the one my mum used. I sprinkled it in and let it cook, simmering gently. Then I beat the eggs and lemon juice until they were frothy and added a ladleful of the stock, whisking like mad. Next I put the mixture into a bigger bowl and added the stock, a little bit at a time. I did that until I had about two thirds of the stock and rice remaining in the saucepan. I let that cool off a little and went the other way, adding the lemony egg mixture to the saucepan. It looked exactly as Mum's *avgolemono* does, but without the little pieces of chicken floating in it. I added salt and pepper—simply because I've learnt to follow recipes to the letter. With my anosmia I can't taste the difference. Serve at once, the recipe book said, and I did that too.

I felt instantly better, or so I told myself. Some things transcend racial and cultural borders: chicken soup is one of them.

Torment

I was surprised to receive an invitation to Nikos's son's wedding. He said, 'It was nothing to do with me, Eleni insisted we invite you. She said you've been a great comfort to her and that it would be a shame to leave you out of our celebration.'

It was a lovely wedding, lots of dancing and laughter. I was seated with the family who run our local milk bar, an elderly couple and their spinster daughter. Some might say that they would not be the most interesting people to spend the evening with, but I always find that if you don't fill up the air talking about yourself and take an interest in others, everyone has a story to tell. I'd known the family for many years, but only tonight learned Maria, the spinster's story. She told me she had been engaged to an Italian, who she loved with all her heart, but a few days before their wedding he called it off.

'I thought I would die of not only a broken heart, but of shame,' she said.

'What are you talking about?' her mother yelled from across the table, over the music. 'This is a wedding, not a funeral, don't look so serious.'

'How long ago was it?' I asked, nodding and smiling at the old woman.

'Twenty years,' Maria said, 'and I still think about him.'

'No one else came along in all that time?'

'No, no one else. Not for me.' She took a sip of retsina and continued. 'He married a good Catholic girl less than a year later, exactly the type of girl his mother wanted as a daughter-in-law. But he cried when he broke it off with me,' Maria said. 'I remember asking him, *why did you ask me to marry you in the first place?* He said he thought he could stand up to the pressure from his family, that they would stop objecting to the marriage once they got to know me. But he said that it was getting worse, and that his mother's blood pressure was critically high. She had begged him to break it off with me, before he killed her.'

I was thinking about family interference and how quickly love can be taken away when I accidentally overheard Chrissie declare her love. Eureka! The child is in love with Nikos's son, George. As soon as I overheard the truth, I scolded myself for not seeing it sooner. As obvious as the mole on the bride's face: Chrissie is tormented with love for her first cousin, a terrible sin in our culture.

'Chrissie it's me,' said the voice at the other end of the phone.

'George!' I hadn't seen or spoken with him since the wedding, and my humiliation in front of the portaloos, several weeks earlier. I still went red at the thought of what an idiot I'd made of myself.

'I wanted to ask you a favour.'

'Sure, anything.' God I was pathetic.

'I've been trying to get a meeting with the head cosmetics buyer at Myer.'

'Julie Smith?'

'That's the one,' said George. 'I've rung twice and left messages, but she hasn't returned my calls.'

'She's very busy, don't take it personally George.'

'I need to get *Nectar of the Gods* into one of the big department stores. Can you help?'

'I thought you wanted to keep it as a boutique brand.'

'We do, but we also need a certain volume of sales.'

'Julie's a pretty tough cookie,' I said.

'Would it be too much to ask you to organise a coffee meeting between the three of us?'

'You and Dora and Julie?'

'No, you and me and Julie,' George said.

'What about Dora?'

'Dora's back in Greece, sorting out some things.'

'OK, I'll talk to Julie and call you back.'

After I hung up I stood in the hallway and pictured George's face. Hearing his voice brought back all the feelings I had for him. Not that they'd really gone away. You only had to scratch the surface of day to day distraction to see that the way I felt about George was right there, covered only by a fine layer of life's dust that could be blown away by a simple two minute conversation.

In the weeks following his marriage to another woman, I had resolved to shake off the misplaced feelings I had for my cousin, for good, by making more of an effort with James. He was clearly my future. I planned a romantic weekend away with my boyfriend to the peninsula, where we made love three times in two days. I told myself I loved James, yet here I was picturing George's face and imagining my hands all over him, and I mean *all* over him. God what was wrong with me? I was perverted, weird, freakish. Dora's being in Greece made my mind race. Could I get him into bed while she was away, and break up their marriage?

'Chrissie, you're drunk,' George's words echoed in my head. Coffee, then wine, and then a hotel room, my other side suggested. It seemed my mind had a mind of its own. I was so excited at the prospect of seeing him without Dora, that the next day I immediately found Julie Smith and persuaded her to meet with George and I the following day.

'A ten minute coffee meeting, Jules,' I said, trying to butter her up, and promising to prioritise the in-store cosmetic displays next season. Then I went and got my hair trimmed, my legs waxed, and my moustache bleached. The morning of the coffee meeting, I dressed carefully in a skirt I knew made me look at least two kilos lighter and I made sure to wear pink lipstick. Pink is for love, red is for lust, a woman who read colours had once told me. Ask me who the Prime Minister of Greece is and I couldn't tell you, but this rubbish, I remember. I really was superficial.

'Can I come for coffee too?' asked Jerry, after I got back from the loo. I'd been anxious all morning, like I was going for a job interview. At the back of my mind I thought, what? That he'd see me again and finally realise he loved me? Logically, I knew I was being ridiculous, but on some other level I sensed that George and I were meant to be together.

'Why do you want to be there?' I asked Jerry.

'To observe,' he said with a look that made me laugh.

'Find your own unrequited love scenario,' I said, grabbing my bag.

George was already sitting in the café when I walked in. He stood up and kissed me on the cheek. God he was gorgeous. 'Julie'll be here in a few minutes,' I said.

'Thanks for arranging this,' said George. He wore a shirt and sports jacket with clean jeans. His hair was cut shorter. His wedding band caught my eye like a hook. I thought of a poem by my favourite Greek poet, Yannis Ritsos.

We have not come together in two months.

A century

and nine seconds.

'So how are you, and how's James?'

'Fine. You?'

'All good.' Then Julie Smith arrived and we ordered coffee and muffins. George gave her his spiel about the products, then produced a lip balm and a pot of cream. Julie smeared both on her wrist and sniffed.

'Nice,' she said, putting them into her designer handbag. 'Tell you what, why don't you send me some figures, costs, sales projections, you know, and also any marketing ideas you have. I'll think about what we can do at our end. I'm sure Chrissie can work her magic with a killer display. I'll talk to my team and give you a call.'

'Thanks,' George said, shaking Julie's hand, as she stood to leave.

'No promises,' said Julie, 'but I have a feeling all this natural stuff is really going to take off in the next few years. I heard on the grapevine that the UK's Body Shop are expanding to Australia this year.' She left and George sat back, beaming. Then without warning he reached over and touched my cheek.

'You've got a muffin crumb … just here.' His fingertips brushed against my skin and I closed my eyes, for a moment, involuntarily. In that morsel of time I felt the soul crushing pain of *what if*. What if it could have worked out for the two of us. What if I'd been brave enough to tell him how I felt before his wedding day? What if I'd dared to kiss him at *Countdown*? Or that time when we were teenagers playing spin the bottle? It was the dull pain of regret: and I was only twenty-six years old.

I drained the last mouthful of my coffee. I had to get out of there before I started to cry. 'Drop by sometime, if you're ever in Prahran,' I said.

'Yeah. Or you and James visit us. You know the address.' Me and James, do something together? We'd already had our outing together for this year.

That night, my lustful dreams resurfaced. We were walking along the beach, George and I when a storm came through. I could see the dark, charcoal blue sky and the deep green of the water. George held his arm across my back, protecting me from the elements, as we hurried towards safety (a tree or a car or a house, I couldn't say). When we stopped, I felt his damp t-shirt and the form of his body underneath it against me. Gritty sand stuck to the back of his neck where he had applied sunscreen and every grain held a world of meaning. We looked at one another and smiled. His hair was wet and dark strands caressed his face. He held me close, then kissed me gently on both cheeks, up high near my eyes. There was no talking in the dream, although the sound of the wind and my heartbeat surrounded us. My longing for him was fiercer than the weather. I looked into his amber coloured eyes. He was a moment away from kissing my lips, when I felt the tide pulling me away. A dog barked, in the dream or was it outside of my window? I struggled to hold onto the feeling of being with George, to the comfort and warmth of holding him, but I was washed into consciousness, and into bed, next to James.

I wanted to find that dog and kick it.

Trouble

I saw Mrs Evans and her dog on High Street today.

'Our newlyweds seem to be having a hard time of it,' she said.

'Who?'

'George,' she said, 'and that girl from Greece.'

'Dora,' I replied.

'They're living with Mr Nikos and his wife, saving money for a home of their own,' she said. 'A bit peculiar if you ask me.'

I should have left right then, walked away quickly with a smile and a *good morning*, but I couldn't. I had to know what she knew. The old lady continued, 'I saw her, the Greek girl, coming home alone a few nights ago. Very late it was too.' I nodded, encouraging her to go on. 'I looked at the clock and it was one in the morning,' she raised her eyebrows. 'I'm not normally up at that time but Trudi had yelped in her sleep and woken me. Then I saw the light come on in their room, across the hall from where Mr Nikos and Eleni sleep.'

'Go on,' I said, keeping a straight face.

'I couldn't really hear anything, but not five minutes later George burst out of the house. Fit for tying he looked. I had the lights off, so I got a good look at his face. I thought I'd wait and see what time he got home.'

'And?'

'I couldn't say, to be honest,' Mrs Evans said. 'I went to bed shortly after. I'm not one for late nights you know.'

'I see.'

'Well, cheery-bye Dearie, can't stand talking all day.'

How my mind raced after that conversation. Was there anything I could do to rid George of Dora, and help Chrissie win him over? But even if Dora were out of the picture, the fact remained that first cousins cannot be together in this way. What shame it would bring to both families, Nikos and Eleni, as well as Voula and her husband. It simply isn't right. I know that and yet I'm aching to see them together, to interfere.

What is to be done with me? For so many years now I've kept to myself and lived silently. I've listened to everyone else, read their cups and dispensed ambiguous advice. Most people know what to do, inside of themselves, where their true self lies. Should I marry the butcher? Will I try for another child? Is my husband cheating on me? I steer them with my readings to their own truth. It's not so difficult. People are transparent, no matter the surface they present to me and to the rest of the world. But now—I'm worse than Mrs Evans and my sister.

Dora was back, like a bout of herpes, from her business trip to Greece, and had come into the department store to see my display for *Nectar of the Gods*. Things had moved surprisingly quickly in the time she was away. One of our regular brands had gone into liquidation and Julie Smith decided that *Nectar of the Gods* would be perfect to slot into their place.

'You've really outdone yourself this time Honey,' Jerry said, 'the window looks amazing.'

'These products will sell themselves,' said Dora. 'Once people try them they will recognise the quality and medicinal properties.'

'Wow, the display looks fantastic!' said George turning up

unexpectedly. He shook Jerry's hand and kissed both Dora and I on the cheek.

'I thought you were meeting that magazine editor today,' said Dora.

'I did. It wasn't a long meeting.' It was September school holidays and George was spending every minute getting *Nectar of the Gods* up and running as a business.

'I hope you talked him into doing a story about our products,' she said, 'we can't afford their advertising rates.'

'Everything's sorted, we've come to an agreement,' said George.

'What does that mean?'

'Let's talk about this later Dora,' George said, smiling at Jerry and I.

'You haven't promised him anything without talking to me first,' Dora said.

'I'm well aware that I'm in debt up to my eye balls Dora, no need to remind me.'

'*We're* in debt, George,' Dora responded in Greek, 'We are in this together, we're married, remember?' Did she think I wouldn't understand.

'I'm not the one who sometimes forgets they're married,' George said, switching to Greek himself.

'Come on, don't start again George, I told you I couldn't find a taxi that night.'

'Never mind, my love,' George said, suddenly changing tack.

'Don't, *my love* me now, after all those accusations,' Dora said. 'Sometimes I think I should have known better than to marry a foreigner.'

Jerry looked at me quizzically and we both shuffled a few feet away, but still within hearing range.

'I hate to tell you,' George said, 'but you're the foreigner here, not me.'

'And I feel like one every minute I'm in this ridiculous country,' Dora hissed. 'All this false politeness, all the pleases and thank yous, and then behind your back, these Australians, who knows what they are saying.'

'No one's saying anything Dora.'

'No? So everyone in this country is perfect,' she sneered. 'I didn't realise I'd emigrated to utopia.'

I called my mother straight after work that day, to get the inside scoop on George and Dora.

'Oh it's you Chrissie,' said Mum breathlessly, 'I've just come in from the garden, you should see how well the parsley is doing this year.'

I interrupted before she could give me a run down on the growth pattern of each and every vegetable and herb in her garden. 'How's things Mum?' I asked. 'And how are George and Dora going?' I wanted dirt, and lots of it. There was trouble in paradise and I couldn't wait to hear all about it.

'How should I know,' my secret source said, 'I don't really see them. It's not like they visit me. Why don't you call your cousin and ask how he is?'

'But has Aunt Eleni said anything to you?'

'Your Aunt Eleni says lots of things. She said Tina seems more cheerful lately,' Mum said. 'She has always been such a serious child.' It seemed things were working out between Tina and the new guy she vaguely told me about; but much as I liked my cousin, I really wasn't all that interested in discussing her well being right at the minute.

'But has Aunt Eleni said anything about Dora?' I was losing patience.

'Chrissie, you never call your parents, and then you finally pick up the telephone and you don't even ask how your father and I are.'

'So how are you Mum?'

'We are very well … thank you for asking. And you?'

'Just terrific.'

Drama

Gossip is buzzing all over Little Greece this week, like bees around a hive. Mrs Evans was so excited she knocked on my door and came in for a cup of tea. After a little small talk she came straight out with it. 'George's wife left him,' she said with a little gleam in her eye, 'and I believe she's gone back to Greece.'

Naturally Nikos had told me this already.

'Married for only a few months,' he said, shaking his head. 'Eleni is full of shame. *A divorce, in this family*, she said to me, *what next, an Australian husband for Tina?* She crossed herself and lit a flame in front of our icon of the holy mother—her role model.' Nikos permitted himself a brief smile, but then added more seriously, 'Eleni hasn't left the house for more than a week. And George is even worse.'

'Terrible,' I had said, holding him closer.

'He's lost all the money he invested in that business with the cosmetics. I was worried about that from the start, what does a Greek man know about face creams?' I stroked his hair. 'My son's cheeks have caved in with grief. His wife has left him, and he's bankrupt. Such a tragedy Magdalena.'

And from the other side of the city my sister calls with news about her tenant, Chrissie. I try to sound disinterested, as I do with other gossip, but

I think both she and Mrs Evans can tell that I have become one of them.

'I saw her cousin visiting, just after the Australian boyfriend left the house,' my sister Panayiota said on the phone. 'First cousins! I hate to think what's going on there. It's a sin against God.'

On top of all this, today, a letter from Greece from Stavros's lawyers. His mother died—God rest her soul, 98 years old. She outlived her husband and her son. Their beautiful house on the lake is now mine.

It was James's big night, the opening of his first solo show, in a trendy gallery not far from where we lived. It was a small space with the traditional white walls, like a sugar cube house on a Greek island. In the expansive front window, facing the street and any passing art lover with deep pockets, hung James's largest and most expensive painting, *Abstract Number Nine*. Two hundred dollars per square foot, the price list should have read. A red 'sold' dot next to the painting had catapulted James's mood from excited to euphoric, turning his normally pale complexion blood red. The gallery director held tightly onto his arm like a scab on a wound. She was dressed to the hilt in 80s chic, big hair, stiletto heels and a shiny yellow belt that threatened to cut her in two. I watched her introducing James to the art collectors and company curators who had been invited to his opening. For our part, James and I had invited all our mostly poor friends. James ignored both them and myself completely. At the drinks table I noticed Jerry and my cousin Tina getting along like a house on fire. Jerry had brought Dean Martin with him, who wore a rhinestone collar for the occasion. I walked over to share the joke.

'Honey, your cousin is a scream,' said Jerry. I'd never heard Tina described in that way before.

'I simply said that I prefer Alexis to Krystal,' Tina said. 'Just because I'm a bottle blonde doesn't mean I can't barrack for a brunette.' Jerry almost spilled his drink laughing.

'What on earth are you guys talking about?' I asked.

'*Dynasty!*' They yelled in unison.

'You're joking?' I replied.

'Get with it Sweets,' said Jerry. 'It's the best show on television.' I raised my eyebrows.

'You're not still hooked on *The Young and The Restless?*' Tina screeched. How many drinks had my cousin had?

Jerry looked horrified. 'Grow up!'

Just then James's parents interrupted. 'Great turn out, isn't it? Mrs Black asked without waiting for an answer. She grabbed a wine and walked away quickly. Mr Black winked at me, 'He might become a rich man yet.' I smiled my standard fake smile and reached for another glass of red. Then George appeared at the door. He had the same ghostly look he'd had for the past couple of months, but at least he'd left the house. I dared to hope he was getting over the gift, Dora. I hated what she'd done to him.

'Hey, look who's here,' I said cheerily, walking over quickly and kissing George on the cheek. Surely a person had no right to look so sexy when they were going through a personal crisis. I brazenly took his hand and showed him around the exhibition. My actions would appear to anyone looking on as sisterly concern. I had everyone fooled. Even Mum had called to tell me how grateful Aunt Eleni and Uncle Nick were that I'd been looking out for George. It made me feel a little guilty. I was enjoying his reliance on me, the calls at night and the visits on weekends. George and I had become closer than ever, but my feelings were still less than familial.

'Just a few words from the artist,' announced the gallery director. James took the microphone and began talking about his primary school art teacher, Mr Waters. This was going to be a long one.

'Speeches always remind me of my wedding,' George whispered. I touched his arm sympathetically. Then to my utter surprise he moved closer and held his arm across my back. I felt the heat from his open palm through the thin cotton top I was wearing. Slowly George's hand began to move, forming small circles. God that felt good. Not sleazy, I told myself, cousinly affection.

'And last but not least, thank you to my partner Chrissie,' I stood rigid, smiling back at James. People turned to look at me. George quickly moved his hand away. 'For all your support and understanding. I know it hasn't been easy, with my disappearing to the studio every weekend.' No, not easy, I thought, just the best part of my week. And with that my transition was complete: Surface Girl was now The Woman with Two Faces.

Unity

My sister came over for lunch with her husband on the weekend. After eating, her better half left for the *kafenio*, to have an ouzo and a cigarette. Minutes later, Mrs Evans came by and I invited her in.

'You must try a Greek coffee,' I said, leaving her with Panayiota in the good sitting room. By the time I came back they had become best friends.

'Magdalena, what do you think?' Panayiota asked me. 'Me and Gladys, we think that somehow those kids must get together. I've had second thoughts about George and Chrissie being cousins. God forgives everything.'

'Terribly romantic isn't it?' Mrs Evans replied. 'Like Romeo and Juliet, right on our doorstep.'

'Or Helen of Troy and Paris,' said my sister the classics scholar.

'James is very handsome,' said Mrs Evans, 'But George doesn't lag too far behind.'

'And a much nicer person,' said my sister. The two women nodded conspiratorially to one another.

'How do you know?' I asked.

'I see him when he visits his cousin, next door,' she said, 'he always smiles and says *Kalimera*. Even when he's unhappy, he's always polite.' She had a very self satisfied look on her face after that.

I put the tray down and poured us each a glass of water. 'Let's see if our cups hold any answers,' I said. Heavens how I longed to discuss it all with them, confide all I knew, but then I'd have been giving my own secret away.

'*Stin-iyamas*, to our health,' said my sister.

'Bottoms up,' said Mrs Evans.

Several months had passed since Dora and her mole had returned to Greece. After the initial shock and heartache, George told me he had come to realise that they should never have got married in the first place. 'It was a holiday fling that went too far,' he said on the phone. 'As soon as we were married, it all started going downhill.' I was glad that he was more or less back to his old self, cheerful and fun. But he still made my heart race. That side of things hadn't changed. I was living with one man, and in love with another—that I could never be with. Something had to be done, a change made, somehow. But for the time being I had other things to think about. My birthday was coming up and as a self absorbed only child I had a series of events planned:

dinner with my parents one night, a big work lunch with Jerry and some others mid week, and to round the week off, a party at our place on the Saturday night.

I made trays of Ritz Crackers with all sorts of visually interesting toppings for the party: slices of tomato with tiny flowers made of olives, blobs of homemade eggplant dip crowned with basil leaves and piped swirls of avocado mush over a smear of vegemite. Clearly I had too much time on my hands and sadly (given my degree in fine art), cooking had become my only creative outlet.

I put on the new Roxy Music CD and drained my second glass of wine, then suddenly panicked about the booze. People would bring their own, but I should have got some extra bottles—just in case.

'Your parents would be ashamed if they knew you weren't supplying all the alcohol,' said George. He was right. Hospitality is a matter of pride for Greeks. The word for hospitality *filoxenia*, means 'friendship with strangers'. If you welcome strangers, what would you not do for your friends?

'So how much have you had to drink?' I asked George, eyeing the stubby in his hand.

'This is my first.'

'Great, you can drive me to the bottle shop. We'll be back before anyone notices.'

A short time later, we pulled out of the local drive through, with a dozen bottles of VB, two litres of orange juice and an enormous bottle of vodka. I had the window wound down and was enjoying the breeze and the anticipation of a drunken night with myself as the centre of attention. Then just two streets away from home, a car failed to stop at the *Give Way* sign and almost hit us. George swerved and

I felt the car lurch in the wake of the other vehicle. I reached out for the dashboard to steady myself. It felt like they missed us by inches. The car honked its horn and kept driving, but George pulled over and turned off the engine.

'Oh my God,' I said. I felt breathless and I was shivering. George leaned over and rubbed my arm. We sat in silence, catching our crazy thoughts. Newspaper headlines ticker taped across my brain, *Girl dies on her birthday*. I moved closer to my cousin George and we hugged. Just as in my dream, I had my cheek pressed against George's face and my fingers through his hair. His breath against my cheek made my longing for him simply unbearable. I reached across and rubbed my fingertips across the stubble on his chin as I had wanted to do since the morning at the airport. I didn't care if this was wrong. Now I had my hands on him, alone and in the dark, I simply couldn't, didn't, want to let go.

'Chrissie,' he whispered. The tenderness in his voice gave me goose bumps. Could it be that what I had suspected was true? That I wasn't the only one who felt the desire between us. And then in Greek like a secret language between lovers, George said, '*Agape mou*, my love.' His kiss felt as inevitable as morning following night. His hands were all over my face and then my arms and breasts. I thought I would die if he stopped. To use an Aussie expression, we went at it like hammer and tongs. I didn't think about James, my parents, his parents, curses or eternal damnation from the church. True passion exists in the moment. Afterwards, well that's a different story.

'We'd better hurry back,' George said, adjusting his clothes. He looked into the rear-view mirror and wiped his lips with a chequered handkerchief. At the house, he carried the booze into the kitchen, while I rushed to my room to reapply my lipstick. I was running a brush through my hair when James walked in.

'Where have you been?' he asked. 'I've been answering the door and telling everyone you're in the backyard.'

'Sorry Darling, I just dashed out for more beer. I didn't think people would be arriving just yet.'

'No, who would think to arrive on the time stated on the invitation?' With that he left the room. Phew. I looked at my face in the mirror. My eyes shone brightly. I'd surely never looked this good. I felt reckless, exhilarated and truly alive.

A crowd of people rushed over when I walked into the living room. One of them was Jerry. 'Happy birthday Honey, you look gorgeous,' he said. He and Tina had apparently arrived together. For a moment I felt hurt, like I was losing my best friend to my cousin. But I was soon distracted by other faces and by presents. Through it all, my eyes found George and I smiled. When he smiled back I thought I'd explode with joy. We kept our distance during the party. I couldn't say who I spoke to, everyone and no one. I opened cards and presents, I drank lots of vodka and ate almost nothing. Despite my drunkenness, every so often I scanned around for George. I saw him dancing with Tina, but mostly he hovered in the kitchen getting drinks for people.

'What's up with your life-of-the-party cousin?' James asked me.

'What, who?' I played dumb.

'He's got lipstick on his collar but he hasn't been near anyone except his sister,' said James. 'Now that's weird!'

'Honestly James, you're so straight sometimes, and you call yourself an artist.' I made inverted comma signs with my fingers. 'A little incest never hurt anyone. By the way, I think I saw your sister looking for you.' Did I really say that? Is alcohol an excuse or was I simply sabotaging our relationship?

'Chrissie, that is too much, even from you!'

'I'm just joking.'

'Well I'm going. You've hardly spoken to me all night, and now you're insulting me.'

'James, don't sulk.' I called after him. But I didn't run after him. I was kind of glad he'd left and made a beeline for George. I took his hand, flirting like mad. 'Your collar's dirty, Georgie.' In fact the smear of colour perfectly matched my crimson lips. I hadn't thought to put on a different shade.

Suddenly James was back; seems he hadn't quite left. He looked from me to George and back again. 'I don't fucking believe it!' he said, storming out. I heard the front door slam. This time I didn't even bother to call out after him.

When James left me he took not only everything that was his, but also everything that was ours. I guess he felt he had it coming, after what I did. He took all the big things like the television and the refrigerator, and he took many of the small things like the pegs from the clothesline and the flowers from the garden. It's true, he did most of the gardening, but when I'd left for work Monday morning, the front garden was covered in purple and pink Cosmos. When I returned, it was a patch of stalks. I had expected repercussions after my party, especially when he didn't return home on the Sunday. But wasn't it a little odd to leave without a fight or a chance to reconcile? On the front porch there were tell tale rings of dirt where pot plants had once stood. They reminded me of tiny crop circles. The aliens had come and gone. I didn't call the police. Ever the polite private school boy, James had left me a note: *Chrissie, Clearly you are in love with your cousin. Good luck with that, James.*

What little sleep I had the week following James's departure was full of dreams. I dreamt about my grandmother, Dad's mother, the one I'm named after. In the dream she presented me with a pair of gold earrings. When I awoke I remembered what my mother had told me all those years ago: a gift of earrings means a girl. It was theoretically possible that I was pregnant. But surely it was unlikely: once, with no protection.

James was scrupulous with his use of condoms. He had premonitions of diseases of the nether regions. Imagining himself like so many great painters before him, Manet, Gaugin and Toulouse-Lautrec who died of Syphilis. I never had the heart to tell him that since the advent of penicillin, it was a treatable disease.

George and I had not discussed birth control. It was not a conversation either of us would have ever deemed necessary. I remembered the passion of our one encounter. Now that was the way to conceive a child, urgently. But what manner of creature might I be carrying? I knew enough about genetics to be scared. I couldn't help but think that my mother's curse was finally coming to fruition. 'May you have a child that causes you as much difficulty as you've caused me.'

I was mad with confusion. On the one hand I wanted to bonk George's brains out, but on the other, I didn't want to speak to him. One minute I thought we could work it out, that it wasn't so bad. Then the next I envisioned myself old, childless and living with twenty cats. I saw people pointing at me and saying, 'That's the weird woman who had ten miscarriages then went crazy and killed her husband. They say they were brother and sister.'

I needed time to think. Thank goodness for answering machines. I screened all my phone calls. For two days no one rang. I busied myself rearranging what was left of the furniture, spreading a handful of pieces throughout a five room house. Enforced minimalism. I bought a small esky to keep the milk in, until I bought another fridge. On the third day George left a brief message, 'Hi Chrissie, I think we need to talk. Call me.' I stood still, barely breathing as I listened to his voice. I felt guilty for being there and not answering. But I didn't dare move because a part of me wanted to lift the receiver and yell, 'I'm here, come over and ravage me!' Two days after that he left three messages. Then the next day there were no messages but seven hang-ups.

The worst part of it all was that my dreams of George and I together had stopped. It appeared that our real life encounter had put an end to them. I missed seeing him at night and I also missed having James around, more than I thought I would. I had wanted change in my life, but not all at once. Going to work was the only thing that kept me on track. Jerry listened with saintly patience and best of all offered no advice but, 'Take it easy on yourself Honey.'

Delusion

For two whole weeks Nikos had not come to see me, and when he finally did, all we did was talk. As a young girl and for most of my life I'd been warned that all men were interested in was sex. What a surprise then, at the age of fifty-two to realise that in fact, that was all I was interested in.

'I'm worried about George and Chrissie,' Nikos said, taking off his jacket and draping it over the back of a kitchen chair.

'Let's go into the sitting room,' I said, 'it will be more comfortable there.' I pictured Nikos and I making love on the couch, something we had never done before.

'The kitchen is fine,' he said.

'Why are you worried?' I asked. I didn't want to give Chrissie away.

'Something is going on there, between those two,' Nikos said, playing with his moustache and drawing attention to his sensuous mouth.

'Is it?' I asked, looking at him longingly.

'They have always been close. When they were younger it was always the two of them running off to play together and leaving Tina out. But now, it's something else.' He ran his fingers through his hair. 'I can hardly bring myself to say it, but I think they are in love. In a romantic way. I suspect George at least is in love with Chrissie.'

'So you're worried, because it's a sin, because they are first cousins,' I said reaching for his hand.

'It's more complicated than that,' Nikos said wearily. He got up and walked about the room. I knew enough to stay silent. Finally he spoke. 'They are not first cousins,' Nikos said, turning to look at me. I didn't know what to say and kept perfectly still. After a few moments he continued. 'In fact they are not related by blood at all. George is Yanni's son.'

'Yanni?'

'My best friend, who was engaged to Eleni,' Nikos said. 'On the trip, coming out to Australia, I told you that Yanni was killed, but what I didn't tell you was that before that tragedy George was conceived—on the ship.' He looked up at me and I noticed how grey his moustache was becoming. 'By the time we docked in Port Melbourne, Eleni was vomiting every day, twice a day or more. Everyone thought she was sea sick, but when her sickness continued on dry land … well, I married her right away.'

'And who knows about this …' I hesitated, looking for the right word, 'about this … situation?' I asked.

'Now, with you included, there are three of us who know,' he responded.

'What are you going to do? Are you going to tell George?'

'How can I tell him now?' said Nikos. 'We should have told him years ago, but Eleni was against it. She always said it was her honour at stake.'

'You could explain the circumstances,' I said. 'No one would think less of her.'

'If we tell George now, he will feel lied to.' Nikos stood up and began pacing around the kitchen again. 'I couldn't love him more you know, his father was the best friend I ever had. George is no different to me than Tina. They are both my children.'

'But what about your niece Chrissie?' I asked. 'I agree with you, I believe the child has strong feelings for George, too, and my sister tells me her boyfriend has moved out of their home.'

'Saints above it's worse than I thought,' Nikos said. 'But what can I do Magdalena? Destroy my family, humiliate my wife? I have to keep silent. It's a shame George's marriage to Dora didn't work out. But eventually they will both find happiness with someone else.'

A week after the incident in the car, I was in my pyjamas putting on super strength night time moisturiser when the doorbell rang. All the crying I'd been doing was accelerating the ageing process. Small lines were rapidly appearing around my eyes. I was like a dried out leaf, soon I would be dust. Looking into the mirror I saw my face drop when the doorbell sounded. Would James ring the bell? After all he still had a key.

'Chrissie, open up!' The voice was muffled, but it wasn't James. 'Talk to me Chrissie.' My heart pounded. I sat on the bed. Next I heard loud banging. We Greeks can be hot headed but surely he wouldn't break down the front door? 'Chrissie, we have to talk.' I didn't want to talk. I wanted to sweep it under the carpet and forget about it. Pretend it never happened, like any other one night stand.

When the knocking stopped my ears strained to hear what was coming next, but it seemed George had gone away. I was both relieved and disappointed. I put the night cream away and wondered how I'd get to sleep. Moments later I heard an almighty crash. 'Shit!' I flew out of my room, down the hallway and into the kitchen. When I turned on the light the first thing I saw was a brick in the middle of the floor, and glass everywhere. George was at the window. He had bundled his t-shirt around this arm and was smashing what remained of the glass, trying to climb through the frame, bare chested. When he saw me he yelled.

I said window.

It was not.

All windows

Open towards you.

Who else but George would simultaneously smash a window and recite poetry?

'George! What the hell are you doing?' I asked, even though what he was doing was blindingly obvious.

'I'm desperate. You won't see me, speak to me. I'm going crazy.'

'Crazy? You're drunk as well.'

'Hey, where's your fridge?' said George suddenly, in a much calmer voice. The esky on the floor was like a skinny understudy standing in for a statuesque actor.

'James took it.'

'What do you mean?'

'He took all his stuff and left me. I haven't seen him since the party.'

'Chrissie, that's great!' He came closer, but I backed away. My slippers crunched glass underfoot.

'George, what happened in the car was a mistake. We're cousins, first cousins.'

'It didn't feel like a mistake to me,' he said. Then added, 'So we won't have any children. I can live with that.'

'What about our parents? Your dad, my mum? They're brother and sister for God's sake. They'll freak.'

'Stuff them. I don't care. I love you Chrissie, and I think you love me too,' George said. 'Hey, let's get away from everyone, we can go to Greece! You'll love it there.'

'You're nuts, you know that?' I said as sternly as I could. He looked so cute in his drunken madness. We stood silently for a while, there didn't seem to be anything else to say. George looked down at the floor. If he cried or suggested any other way out of our ridiculous situation I didn't know what I'd do. I was a heartbeat away from rushing over to him.

'I'll help you clean this up and then I'll go,' he said finally. My heart sank. I grabbed a broom and dustpan. While George swept up I called a 24 hour glazier, who arrived within minutes and replaced the glass quickly and efficiently. He didn't make chit chat or ask any questions. I suppose he saw lots of domestic disputes. Bricks through windows were probably his bread and butter work. When I went to my room to get my purse, George left, hopping over the fence to the lane that ran out the back of the house, the way he'd come in.

'Your ... friend already paid me,' said the glazier. 'Here's your receipt ... and my card, in case you need me again. Goodnight.'

Alone I sat on the esky and cried like I'd never cried before, washing away the expensive night cream that I'd only just applied. Then I turned off the kitchen light, went to bed and cried some more.

Change

We meet less frequently now, me and Nikos, which makes the occasions that we do, all the more passionate. What a force sex is, like a hurricane sweeping your logical mind away. But I would be lying if I said that being together physically was all that was between us, for I miss him very much between visits and I long to share more with him than just a bed. It seems I have stupidly fallen in love with another woman's husband. What is to be done now? Either he leaves his wife, something that I would find difficult to live with, or we stop seeing one other—equally difficult. I should have known it couldn't keep going as it was. Nothing ever remains the same: love dies or is born, people change, circumstances alter. I was self contained and now I am open to heartache. Heaven help me.

On top of everything I am worried about Chrissie. I haven't seen her for several weeks. I want to tell her that she and George can be together, that she needn't suffer, but I can't betray Nikos. What a muddle she and I are both in.

The 'melan' in melancholy means blue black, like ink, in Greek. That had been my mood for weeks. The only thing that took my mind off the pain of not being with George, was cooking. There was also the niggling matter of pregnancy. My period was only a couple of days late, but what with dreams, curses and possible genetic complications, I knew I'd have to do a test sooner or later.

I rushed through Prahran market, looking for inspiration for dinner. It was only half an hour until closing. I was definitely in the mood for something black. I toyed with the idea of making tapenade with Kalamata olives but then came across the fishmongers and decided on squid, cooked in its own ink: perfect. I rushed home with my plastic bag of ingredients. Unfortunately for me, Mrs Xanthos was in her front garden, watering the tomato plants when I got home. I waved a quick hello and thought I'd made it safely through until I felt her hand on my arm.

'Just a moment my dear,' Mrs Xanthos said, clutching me tightly. 'I wanted to make sure you were all right.' She had a surprisingly strong grip for an old lady. 'I heard a terrible sound the other night, like a window breaking. Are there any repairs you need my husband to make?'

'No, everything is fine.'

'Sure?' she said in English, for emphasis.

'It must have come from the laneway,' I said, disentangling my arm. 'Drunks smashing beer bottles. Good-bye.'

Inside the house I stood still for a minute and breathed deeply. I'd certainly got off lightly there. In the kitchen I first washed my hands and then the rubbery body of the calamari; which I cut into rings and left to drain on the sink. Then I sautéed onions with plenty of garlic, oregano and a bay leaf. I had a small branch from my mother's tree that I kept in a vase the way some people keep dried flowers. Then I added a can of chopped tomatoes and a quarter of a cup of white wine. I poured myself a generous glassful for good measure and turned on the oven.

Next came the tricky part. I slit the ink sacs and squeezed the ink into a bowl, to which I added a little water. I poured this dark mixture into a casserole dish together with the squid and onion mixture. When it was in the oven, I poured myself another white wine. Forty-five minutes later the kitchen timer went off. I awoke with a start. I'd fallen fast asleep on the couch.

I went into the kitchen, took the casserole out of the oven and sprinkled chopped parsley onto the dish—an offering to my melancholy. I then wondered whether there was a Greek God of sadness. Athena had wisdom, Aphrodite covered beauty. It had to be a woman with out of control PMT, I thought to myself as I set the table. I lit a candle and poured another wine. With my stifled palette (apparently 90% of taste is due to smell), beautiful table presentation was essential.

Directly afterwards I cleaned my teeth, called a cab and headed to the street that I grew up in.

Prophecy

I was startled by a knock on my front door at ten o'clock at night. Nikos had come and gone. Who else would visit so late? I'd already changed into my dark blue nightie, the only non-black item of clothing I own. I had looked for a black one after Stavros's death, but they were all the sexy sort: inappropriate for a widow. The knocking was insistent.

'Who is it?' I asked in English.

'It's me, Chrissie.'

'My goodness child, what a time to call.'

'I'm so sorry. I didn't know who else to talk to. Can you please read my cup? It's very important.' She looked pale and had dark circles under her eyes. A bit anaemic, I thought. Possibly pregnant.

'It's late for coffee my dear,' I replied, but Chrissie had a desperate look about her. 'All right, I'll put one cup on for you, but you'll need to cross my palm with silver and gold at this late hour.' As I scooped coffee and sugar into the expensive copper *briki* that I keep strictly for divination purposes, I couldn't help but think how strange it was that uncle and niece often visited within a day of one another. It had to be something to do with ties of blood. People who are related have a sense of one another. I believe that.

'I need advice,' Chrissie said, 'and guidance.' Definitely pregnant. And now that her boyfriend had left her … it was no wonder she was worried, poor child. She drank the coffee so quickly it was a wonder she didn't scald her tongue. As we waited for the cup to drain and the patterns to form she fidgeted around in her seat, went to the toilet and then pulled her chair closer to mine.

'Let's see what your cup has to say,' I said, putting on my glasses and peering inside. I turned it around as I always do, to give myself time to think. Then suddenly I really did see something.

'So you are still alive,' said my mother when I picked up the phone after hearing her voice on the answering machine. 'I called yesterday too, but didn't leave a message.' So she was the one hanging up on the machine. It seemed George had given up on me for good.

'I've been busy,' I said, although I'd never been less busy in my entire life. Apart from going to work I'd hardly been anywhere at all.

'I'm going to make a big tray of stuffed peppers this Sunday, why don't you visit. Your father misses you.'

'Sounds good Mum.'

'What about James, do you think he'll come with you now his exhibition has finished?'

'Probably not,' I said. 'Actually I wanted to talk to you and Dad about James.'

'I hope you are finally getting married. I don't like it that you are living in sin, as the Aussies say.'

'I'll speak to you about it on Sunday Mum.'

'As you wish Chrissie, good-bye.'

That worked out well. I could pop in and see Mrs Mavros before lunch at Mum and Dad's on Sunday. I was a little worried about her. The last time I saw her, when I barged in half drunk at night, she looked thin and drained in that awful blue nightie.

I got off the tram a stop after the usual one and approached Mrs Mavros's house from the next street along. I had no intention of walking past George's house and risking an accidental meeting. I was still haunted by our incident in the car as well as the broken window confrontation. I didn't know what to do, but I did know I had to avoid George at all costs. Walking through Mrs Mavros's back gate, I noticed that all the blinds at the back of the house were drawn, even though it was a lovely day. Closer to the house I heard voices. Someone was with her.

'Come in my child,' said Mrs Mavros opening the back door. And there in the kitchen, sitting on a steel framed chair and dressed for winter in a heavy hand knitted cardigan and sky blue polyester slacks, was Mrs Evans.

'Hello Dearie,' she said. 'Visiting our neck of the woods, are you?' I nodded. 'We're just having a cuppa, would you like one?'

'Thank you, that would be lovely,' I said, feeling like I'd walked into some kind of surreal mad hatters tea party.

'I was just telling young Magdalena here, about the Anzac biscuits I brought over,' she said speaking slowly. For whose benefit, I didn't know. 'These biscuits are our tradition.' Mrs Mavros handed me a cup of tea and took a seat next to Mrs Evans. She seemed distracted. 'You know about Anzac day and the diggers?' Mrs Evans asked, offering Mrs Mavros a biscuit.

'Thank you, yes I've heard of them,' Mrs Mavros said, taking one. But no sooner had she taken a bite, than she started going red in the face, coughing and gasping for breath.

'Did it go down the wrong way?' Mrs Evans asked. 'I'll fetch you a glass of water.'

'Call an ambulance,' Mrs Mavros managed to say, before falling to the ground. I rushed to the phone and dialled 000. There was a buzzing in my ears and my heart raced. When I got back to Mrs Mavros, Mrs Evans was kneeling over her, loosening her black blouse.

'She says she's allergic to honey,' Mrs Evans said. The old lady looked about to cry. 'How was I supposed to know? I didn't know Chrissie.'

I ran to the front door and opened it wide. At the end of the garden path I opened the small gate and looked up and down the street. Where was that ambulance? Dashing back inside to where the two women were, I sat on the floor and put my ear to Mrs Mavros's mouth to hear if she was still breathing. That's when she whispered, 'You and George can be together.' I pulled back suddenly, almost head butting Mrs Evans in the face.

'Steady on,' Mrs Evans said, rising to her feet with a groan. 'What's she saying?'

'I can't make it out,' I lied. It was then we heard the ambulance pull up.

'Out of the way please,' said the paramedic. 'What's happened?' he asked, putting down his bag.

'We think she's allergic to honey,' I replied. Mrs Evans was beside herself by now and unable to speak. The ambulance guy took out a syringe, tapped in twice and jabbed it into Mrs Mavros's limp arm.

In a taxi, on the way to the hospital to drop off a few of Mrs Mavros's things, her choked words spun round my head like a tornado, 'You and George can be together.' So she'd worked out who I was in love with. Well she was a psychic. But surely she knew that as first cousins we couldn't be together. I was painfully tired and more confused than ever.

'No visitors,' said the woman at the information desk.

'Can I leave this bag for her?' I asked, and was dismissed with a nod. I was about to leave the hospital when I remembered I was supposed to be having lunch with my parents. I called Mum from a pay phone in the foyer to tell her what had happened.

'I think I'll just go home now,' I said. 'I'm sorry about lunch.'

'Doesn't matter,' she said, 'your father can take the leftovers to work tomorrow.'

I hung up and turned to leave. Facing me was the place I had been avoiding for weeks: a chemist shop. The universe was telling me that the time had come. I took a deep breath, walked in quickly and bought a pregnancy testing kit.

I'd only been home for two minutes when I heard knocking. What now? I shoved the white paper bag containing the pregnancy testing kit under my doona before answering the front door

'Who is it?' I asked, although I hadn't heard from or seen George for a couple of week.

'It's me, Mrs Xanthos.' I opened the front door. 'I didn't realise you were the nervous type, my girl,' she said. 'You know you can always call me or my husband if you're ever scared at home alone.' Of course she'd noticed that James had moved out.

'Thank you Mrs Xanthos. Can I help you?'

'My sister Magdalena called me from the hospital.'

'How is she?'

'She wanted me to thank you for dropping off her nightgown and toothbrush, and to let you know that she is already feeling much better. In fact the woman doctor said she can leave and go home in a day or two.'

'That's great news.'

'Ever since she was a girl she's had this problem with the honey, and with the bees. She was always the delicate one in our family,' Mrs Xanthos said. 'I'm going to take her home the day after tomorrow and stay for a few days, to make sure she is alright,' she added. 'Well, good-bye.'

I went back into my room, pulled up the doona cover and stared at the white paper bag. The moment of truth had arrived. I nervously opened the chemist's bag, read the instructions on the leaflet inside the box and went to the loo, where I peed on the enclosed stick. Too easy, too private. Shouldn't a person have someone there for this ritual? Not right there in the toilet, but nearby; someone to hug after you've washed your hands thoroughly. 'George, I'm pregnant.' Hip hip hooray. As if my life wasn't complicated enough.

Repair

After a good night's sleep in my own bed, I awoke more clearheaded than I'd been for a long time. I knew exactly what I had to do. Eleni was the one with the secret, Eleni was the one to make things right. And almost as if I'd summoned her through my thoughts, she knocked on my door a few days later, with a plate of home made *paximathia*. Fortuitously, my sister was over the road visiting her new best friend, Mrs Evans.

'These will be lovely with a cup of coffee,' I said. 'Do you have time to stay?'

'You sit down,' she said. 'I'll make the coffee.' I watched her in my kitchen, this woman who was the wife of my lover. She was a good person but like so many of us, her life was ruled by things that had been hidden, by secrets.

'Let me read your cup, just for fun,' I said, putting my plan into action. I turned her cup around with two hands. 'It's very busy,' I said in a surprised voice. Eleni leaned towards me to have a look. 'I don't know how I've missed some of this before,' I said.

'What is it Mrs Mavros?'

'A clock.'

'What does a clock mean?'

'It means the time is right.' I looked up at her expectant face and added, 'The time for change.' I pushed my glasses up the bridge of my nose and peered more closely. 'Also, I see two birds—love birds. They are close to you, but something is keeping them apart.' I turned the cup around to show her. 'See here, between the two birds is a wall.'

'I see, I see,' said Eleni, 'but what has it to do with me?'

'There is a wrong for you to make right,' I said. 'Something from a long time ago, something that needs to be said.'

'Christ and Virgin Mary forgive me,' Eleni said crossing herself three times. 'I am a sinner.'

'That's not for me to say,' I told her. 'We are all sinners, after all. But I think your headaches and spells may not be the evil eye.'

'No?'

'It seems to me ... look here,' I pointed, 'on this side the road is clear. Do you see?' Eleni nodded. 'I see a happy and easy life ahead for you, but this wall needs to come down first.' The poor woman looked pale, like she was about to have another one of her turns. 'Naturally I have no idea what any of this means Eleni,' I said, 'the important thing is that *you* know what to do.'

'Thank you Mrs Mavros, thank you.' She stood up to leave, taking out her purse to pay me.

'Not today Eleni,' I said. 'Today has been a coffee between friends. I'm so happy that you came to see me, and please call me Magda.'

Just then there was a loud knocking at my front door.

It was a beautiful early autumn day and so pleasant I almost forgot how unhappy I was. I'd known for a week now that I was pregnant, and that the father was my first cousin George. If moving in with James had upset my parents, this would kill them. And if they were horrified, I could only imagine the reaction from Uncle Nick and Aunt Eleni. She was fragile at the best of times, this would surely send her round the bend. Of course I could 'do' something about the pregnancy. I believed it was a woman's right to choose, but that was in the abstract. Now, when it was my body, my potential baby, it felt different. I had absolutely no idea what I was going to do, and so I thought I'd follow my usual strategy of sweeping it under the carpet; for the time being at least. I was going to eat Chinese food, drink tea and worry about it later. Sensible Chrissie. A cool head in a crisis. Tina had called in the morning and invited me out for a yum cha lunch. I accepted gratefully. 'I have something to tell you face to face,' she had said mysteriously.

When I walked into the restaurant a wave of nausea hit me. Tina was seated at a table set for three. Next to her was my gay friend Jerry, who was so busy nuzzling at Tina's neck and fondling her knee that he didn't notice me coming in.

'I thought you'd be surprised,' Tina said, rising to give me a hug. I noticed straight away that she was wearing a particularly short skirt.

Jerry smiled nervously. 'We wanted to tell you first: since you're the one who introduced us.'

'I hope you're OK with this,' Tina added, touching Jerry's face.

'Sit down Honey, this might come as a bit of a shock, but … I'm straight,' Jerry said.

'What?'

'I'm a closet heterosexual. In fact I had a bit of a crush on you back in college.' He looked smug, glanced at Tina and smiled.

'I thought you were checking out my outfits,' I said.

'Legs,' Jerry stated simply. 'I've always been a fan of the pins.'

This was the funniest and most surprising thing I'd ever heard, and I burst out laughing. It was the best laugh I'd had in weeks. I pulled a tissue out of my bag and wiped my eyes.

'It's not that funny,' said Jerry.

'Yes it is,' Tina and I said together.

'Pork and prawn dumplings?' asked the waitress who had appeared suddenly as if by stealth.

'Yes please,' I said sitting down. Within minutes our table was covered in a plethora of plates. Every dish looked so dainty and pretty that we hadn't been able to say no to any of them: sesame chicken, crunchy vegetarian spring rolls, paper thin parcels of prawn meat and bright green vegetables in oyster sauce. All of it was delicious. As we ate Tina and Jerry confessed their insatiable love for one another.

'I was worried about the age difference at first,' Tina said. 'Jerry's five years younger than me, *and* he's not Greek. But I really had no choice.' Jerry leaned over and kissed her sweetly on the lips. 'I was in love.'

'We were in love,' Jerry corrected her.

'We could not, not be together,' Tina said.

'I still don't know how I'm going to come out to Mum,' Jerry added with a grin. 'My being straight could kill her.'

Tina's face darkened, 'I'm so sorry about you and James.'

'Don't worry,' I said. 'I'm feeling OK. Really. I've got some other things on my mind.' I popped another prawn fritter into my mouth. I couldn't remember the last time I had enjoyed a meal so much. The flavours seemed stronger. Normally, because of my anosmia I only got a general sense of sweet or salty. This was different. Something weird was happening.

We were all quiet and as if to break the silence, Tina asked, 'Have you seen George lately?' As soon as she said his name my head started swimming.

'No,' I said. 'Why?'

'He's been very quiet lately; not himself. I thought he may have called you.'

'No,' I lied again. In fact he had called just the night before, but I still wasn't picking up the phone. I had become accustomed to ignoring its ring and couldn't help but think that this blocking out skill could prove useful, once my sure-to-be-deformed, screaming baby was born.

'What's he up to today?' I asked as casually as I could.

'Don't know,' said Tina looking into Jerry's eyes. She may as well have said, 'Don't care'.

Suddenly I had to get out of there. 'Listen, I've got to go,' I said grabbing my bag and leaving some money on the table. 'Honestly, I couldn't be happier for the two of you.'

Outside the restaurant I stopped, sniffed and smelled oregano and roast lamb. It was astonishing, like running into a wall that hadn't been there a moment ago. I wondered if it had something to do with being pregnant. In a rush I was eight, and in the backyard at Mum and Dad's celebrating Easter with George and his family. The spit roast sizzled as drops of animal fat hit the glowing coals. George and I were tearing pieces off the carcass, burning our fingers and laughing. George: I had to find George.

I'd been cursed by my mother, fallen pregnant by my cousin and now I was risking damnation by the Orthodox Church. This was no Jane Austen, Church of England scenario, where marrying your cousin was considered a good match. I was dealing with Orthodoxy the mother of all Christianity. We saw the Catholics as Johnny-come-latelies. But in my heart, no not just that, in my soul I knew George was the one for me. And if it was my soul that I was risking, then I knew at that moment it was a risk I had to take.

I wandered as if in a daze looking for the tram stop that would take me to George's house. The world was a different place now. There was an extra layer of meaning, which was confusing me. Without quite knowing why, I forgot about the tram and followed the Easter smell. A short block away I found myself in Lonsdale Street, smack bang in the middle of the Greek precinct. A jewellers shop caught my eye. 'A gift of earrings means you'll have a girl.' I touched my belly; a baby, George's and my baby. For an instant I felt happy. This was perfect. This was wonderful. But then I pictured my parents. I saw my mother's shocked face, my father's disapproval, and I felt sick. I had to sit down.

Next to the jewellers was a restaurant, perhaps I could stop in for a short rest and a drink of water. In the window a small animal's worth of meat spun around next to an electric wall of heat. The door was open and bouzouki music blared out together with a charred animal smell. I stood in the doorway dazed and overcome. It appeared as though my nose was in charge now and I had followed it back to my childhood. Waiting for me there, was George. He was sitting at a table in the middle of the room. George, my wonderful, adorable George. He was laughing, looking very George-like. But wait a minute. Why was he looking so happy? If he did truly love me, as he said he did, shouldn't he be in a darkened room listening to The Smiths? He was with someone. I hadn't expected this. The excitement I felt seconds earlier turned into a boulder in the pit of my stomach. I knew right away that I had to get out of there, and fast, before he saw me. This was the worst, the absolutely worst thing that could have happened. While I'd been screening my calls, George had met someone else.

I pushed my way through the lunch time crowd. I looked directly ahead of me, walking as fast as I could, without actually running. But just as I had a built in radar for George, it seems he had one for me too. I heard my name being called, and within a minute I felt his hand on my shoulder.

'Chrissie! Hold on.' He was a little out of breath, but smiling. In fact I'd never seen him smile so widely. I felt like throwing up. 'Chrissie, how are you?' George was positively beaming. I thought he'd give himself a headache he looked so intensely happy.

'Who's your girlfriend?' I asked.

'What are you talking about?'

'The pretty little blonde you were sitting with.'

'I wasn't sitting with anyone,' George said, 'the waitress was about to take my order.' He looked annoyed and I was scared that he'd changed his mind, decided he didn't love me after all. 'Besides, you're the one who said it can't work out between us. You're the one who won't answer the phone, won't open the door.'

'I'm so confused George.' It was true. The overload of aromas had clearly scrambled my brain. A moment earlier I thought I knew what I wanted, now all over again I didn't know what to think.

Later I was to learn that *anosmia* can be reversed by major changes in the body, like pregnancy; but on that first day I was bewildered beyond belief. George and I took a tram back to Thornbury together. We were going to speak to our parents, although I don't think either of us knew exactly what we were going to say. At the Gertrude Street bend, a man taking his last puff of a cigarette hopped on board. When he walked past to take a seat, the smell of him made me gag. And worse still, sitting on the other side of me was a woman whose perfume was giving me a headache. Compounding all of this I had morning sickness and I dreaded the confrontation ahead. I imagined Aunt Eleni fainting, Uncle Nick yelling and my mother and father never speaking to me again. I sat stiffly next to George leaving space on the seat between us. We might have looked like strangers, each with their own thoughts. 'You and George can be together,' Mrs Mavros had said. But how? Without children?—we'd blown that option already. In another country where no one knew we were related?—that seemed a little extreme.

I remembered that since I was a little girl I'd always fallen in love with boys (and later men) who looked entirely different from myself. In grade two it was pasty-faced Rodney Collins; in grade six, the king of pop Johnny Farnham; in high school out of Starsky and Hutch, it was boyishly blonde Hutch that I ached for; and later at college, I was head over heels for front man Sting. My one serious relationship had been with James, who had been nicknamed *snowy* as a child. And now here I was in love with a male version of myself, the closest thing I had to a brother. Was this love akin to narcissism? Or was the blonde phase a period of self loathing?

My mind went back to Mum and Dad, and Uncle Nick and Aunt Eleni. How would they take the news that George and I wanted to be together? And how would George react to my pregnancy? It all seemed like too big a mess to ever be resolved. I felt nervous and sick, and tired. So very, very tired.

I looked up just in time to pull the cord for our stop. On my left was the newsagents on the corner, where I used to pick up *Pink* magazine every fortnight when I was fourteen, and later when I was at college, *Juke* or *RAM*. It was my marker for home. George stood up at exactly the same time. We looked at one another and smiled. Silently he kissed the top of my head.

'Anyone home?' George yelled, opening the front door of his parents' home. No one answered. We walked down the darkened hallway, through the living room and into the kitchen. The whole house was empty and the back door was wide open. Stepping outside we saw Uncle Nick sprawled and smoking on a canvas deck chair, next to some potted plants and a half empty bottle of ouzo.

'What's happening Dad?' George said.

'My boy, my boy and my beautiful girl.' He stumbled over and hugged us tightly. His breath made me take a step back.

'Where's Mum?' George asked.

'With the widow on the corner.'

'Mrs Mavros?'

'The very same,' Uncle Nick said, taking another gulp from the bottle.

'Come on Chrissie,' George said.

Truth

'Is my mum here?' George asked the moment I opened the front door. He was clearly in no mood for niceties like saying hello. I was surprised to see Chrissie with him. She smiled at me weakly as they both came in and I knew that this whole situation was about to resolve itself like a storm blowing itself out. 'We just found Dad at home, sitting alone in the backyard drinking ouzo.'

'Your mother *is* here,' I said, 'come in.' Not a moment later, Nikos appeared.

'Eleni, my wife,' he screamed. 'I love you, but the secrets have to end. They have to end today.' George and Chrissie looked to me, then to Eleni and finally rested upon Nikos. Peering behind him like two budgerigars, one on each shoulder, were Mrs Evans and my sister Panayiota.

'Is this a bad time?' Mrs Evans asked. Panayiota whispered something in her ear and they took a step back.

'I'm in love with Chrissie.' George said suddenly.

'There, I told you,' Nikos said to me.

'When have you been speaking to the widow?' asked Eleni.

'Please everyone, quieten down,' I said, taking charge. 'Panayiota, Gladys, come in. Eleni and Nikos, I suggest you go home and talk with your son. Now excuse me but I need to lie down. I only got out of hospital a few days ago.'

'Yes, yes,' Eleni said, gathering her son and husband like a mother hen with her chicks. As he walked out of my home, perhaps for the very last time, Nikos looked over at me with a sad and poignant look that said, *good-bye.*

It all came to a head at Mrs Mavros's house. No sooner did George and I arrive than Uncle Nick stumbled in, and right behind him my landlady Mrs Xanthos and my old neighbour Mrs Evans. Another wave of nausea hit me when everyone started speaking all at once. If only I could sit down. When Mrs Mavros sent George away with his parents I felt completely alone and abandoned. Where was my mother? Why hadn't we called in there?

'Don't cry my child,' said Mrs Mavros.

'God looks after us all,' said Mrs Xanthos.

'I'll get you a cup of tea,' said Mrs Evans, pulling over a kitchen chair. But before I could sit down, George burst back into the room like a hurricane.

'Chrissie, *agapi mou*, you and I are not cousins after all,' he said. It was then that I fell to the ground in shock, but before any of the ladies could move, George threw himself down next to me, wrapped his arms around me and looked into my eyes. I saw myself reflected back, small and dazed but smiling.

'I've got some news for you too, George,' I said.

Renewal

After so many years in Australia I had forgotten how different the sunlight is in Greece. What a shock my neighbours in Little Greece would have to see me Magdalena Mavros, the widow on the corner, sitting on the beach and wearing a white swim suit. I've kept my figure thank goodness. Nikos always said I could put a twenty year old to shame with my legs and slim waist. Darling Nikos, what a sweet and passionate farewell we had. In the end it was he who encouraged me to follow my instincts and leave Australia.

Not long after Chrissie and George's wedding I sold my corner house and came back to Greece, but not to the town I grew up in, but to Athens. Athens makes Melbourne seem like a village. It's such a crazy and crowded city; and yet I've chosen not to be invisible here. I teach English now. Everyone wants to learn English here in Greece. Some of my students have become friends, and I have coffee with a couple of ladies who live in my apartment block. One of them has recently returned from living in Germany. She understands how sometimes I am homesick for a place that never saw me as a 'real' Aussie. *Then pirazi*, it doesn't matter, I've made my life here now.

On my last day in Melbourne, Mrs Evans took a taxi to see me off from Panayiota's house. 'I have something for you,' I said to the old woman, 'It's my *briki*. Now you can brew your own Greek coffee. Let's go to the kitchen, so I can show you how it's done.' I measured out one small cup of water, a teaspoon of sugar and a heaped spoonful of powdery coffee for each person.

As we waited for the brown mixture to bubble, Mrs Evans said, 'I saw Chrissie and George visiting Voula and Mr Vasili yesterday. She looked very well for a new mother, but I mustn't jinx her.' Then she spat three times, 'Twho, twho, twho,' just like she were one of us. 'You must feel very proud that she named her daughter after you,' she said.

'I may not be a mother, but now I am a *yiayia*,' I said.

'I can still hear that brick going through the window,' my sister Panayiota said, changing the mood; and we all laughed.

'I knew it would all work out in the end. I saw it in her cup,' I proudly told them. 'I said to her, the time she knocked on my door in the middle of the night: you will have a beautiful little girl, and Chrissie asked me, *Will she be all right?*' Panayiota and Gladys nodded and smiled as I finished my story. 'Happy and healthy, I told her.'

'And so it is,' said Panayiota.

'And so it is,' echoed Mrs Evans.

Open for Inspection

Elizabeth took a colour flyer from the well-groomed real estate agent.

'Name and a contact number please?' the woman asked.

'Mrs Smith,' said Elizabeth, then before the woman could ask further, 'Harriet Smith.' Well someone had to actually be named Smith, there were pages and pages of them in the phone book.

It was more a mansionette than a house. Elizabeth passed it every weekday on the bus to work and had often wondered who lived there. Double front doors led into an impressive entrance hall. It was bare except for a large rubber plant and an enormous framed print, the sort they had in cafés. Retro, Elizabeth thought they called them. The house reminded her of a museum, there were Persian rugs and artwork everywhere.

The living room was smaller than Elizabeth might have expected and there was no sign of a television set. It made Elizabeth somehow uncomfortable, but then she found it hidden inside an armoire—like an incontinent aunt in a nursing home. It was books that took pride of place here, an entire wall full of them. Elizabeth glanced at the titles: The Philosophy of Romantic Love, The Shock of the New, and The Andy Warhol Diaries. She pigeonholed the owners easily: arty farty intellectuals. He was probably a lawyer and she was a teacher.

On the side table she stopped to look at a group of frames. If she were selling a home she would be sure to hide such evidence of herself. Seems he had a beard and dark hair, she was blonde, or at least chose to be. Three kids.

In the kitchen the fridge was covered in children's drawings. There was also a photocopied enlargement of a birth notice from *The Age*. 'Welcome to the world baby Chloe (7lb. 7oz.) from mum Helen, dad Henry and your brother and sisters: Ethan, Samantha and Lily.' It was dated from the month before. They were probably looking for a larger home.

To one side of the kitchen was an old style laundry where a clothes horse squatted, burdened with a Hills Hoist's worth of garments, all small. No nappies, she noticed. They probably used disposables, everyone did these days; apparently. On the washing machine was an empty baby capsule, wool lined. It was the sort that locked into a cradle in the back seat of a car. Well they couldn't have gone too far, perhaps having a cup of tea with one of the neighbours, she thought. Elizabeth had a quick peek into the dining room, then started for the stairs.

There was a series of prints along the staircase wall, one atop the other. They were of children's faces, scribbled lines, messy but nice. Elizabeth looked at the signatures at the bottom of each one. They were all by the same artist, H Johnston. Impulsively she went back down the staircase and into the dining room. In her haste, she almost bumped into a couple coming the other way. The woman was conspicuously pregnant. On the large dark wooden table Elizabeth found the sale documents. The vendors were listed as Henry and Helen Johnston. One of them was an artist. How interesting, she thought, looking at all the artwork more closely, as she resumed her tour of the house.

The bedrooms were all upstairs. An ensuite came off one side of the master bedroom. There were pictures in here too. A seascape and three box-like frames displaying shells. The walls were painted green and the towels were a darker shade of the same colour. It was spotless, shiny, perfect. A walk-in closet completed the area; her clothes ran along one side, his along the other. The three room configuration was about the same size as Elizabeth's entire home. Could a bungalow out the back of someone's block be called a home? she wondered. Well whatever it was called, it was all Elizabeth had.

More people had arrived by now, and Elizabeth had to squeeze past a gay couple coming into the closet. Soon there may be male clothes on either side of the wardrobe, she thought. Elizabeth hoped there were some genuine buyers in amongst the sticky beaks like herself. Before going downstairs she stopped to imagine a life such as this. If Charles hadn't been riding that day, on his new aluminium-framed bicycle, would she have had this perfect life? Of course she'd married far too late to have so many children. One would have been nice.

What on earth did people do before Google? Hire private detectives, Elizabeth supposed as she typed in the names and the word *artist*. She looked around, suddenly wary of being in a public library. No one was paying her the least bit of attention. There was a Helen Johnston doing a PhD at Sydney University in art history and a Henry someone or other in Perth who ran an artistic floral arrangement business. The person she was after was towards the bottom of the list: Helen Johnston, Melbourne artist. The pictures on the gallery web site were similar to the ones Elizabeth had seen on the stairway wall, scribbled faces. Hurriedly she read the short biography, then wrote down the name and address of the gallery on the back of her bus ticket. They closed at five. If she caught a cab, she just might make it.

The woman at the gallery was a clone of the real estate agent from that morning, except she wore a brighter shade of lipstick.

'Can I help you with anything?' she asked.

'Yes, I'm interested in the work of Helen Johnston.'

'Are you a friend of Helen's?'

'An acquaintance,' Elizabeth replied without thinking.

'I don't know how she does it,' the woman said. 'A new baby and still finding time to draw. I believe the etchings are on hold for the time being. Acid and babies, aren't a good combination.'

Elizabeth laughed nervously. What was she doing here? She couldn't afford to buy art. She dug her hands deeper into her coat pockets, fingering the frayed edges of the lining. But the gallery woman was already pulling out a number of framed pictures from the storeroom and lining them up against the wall.

'I like these ones best,' she said. 'They have an immediacy that is quite compelling.'

'Yes,' replied Elizabeth. She couldn't draw a straight line, not without a ruler.

'Quite reasonably priced too. I've told Helen she should mark them up. We women undervalue ourselves, don't we?'

'Yes.' Before she dared ask, Bright Lips volunteered the information.

'The larger ones are $900, but the small ones are only $500. They're a steal really.'

'I'll have to think about it.' Elizabeth responded.

The following Saturday, Elizabeth arrived at the house fifteen minutes before it was due to open for inspection. She saw the family leaving on foot, as she'd suspected. The baby was in a double pram, with a sister beside her. Elizabeth couldn't make out Helen's face, it was hidden beneath a wide brimmed hat, but no one would have guessed from her figure that she'd just had a baby. A small child of about four walked behind them, tearing at a slice of white bread. Every now and again she stopped to drop a crumb or two onto the pavement, like she were in a fairytale. Father and son followed a short distance behind.

Elizabeth watched as they turned the corner. She hadn't moved in a herd like that since school. She saw herself then, long hair, no make up, jeans and oversized jumpers. She fancied herself fat at the time. If she'd known then what she knew now, she would have made the most of being a size ten, worn her clothes tighter and her skirts shorter.

Two days before the auction Elizabeth received a small package in the mail. Excitedly she tore open the plastic mail bag. Perhaps I've won something, she thought, or it could be a belated birthday present. It was a free faecal test kit from the Cancer Council; almost a birthday present, for she'd received it precisely because she had recently turned fifty. 'Lucky me,' she said out loud. It wasn't something she'd ever thought to test for, but cancer did frighten her. Her father had died of lung cancer, common enough in men of his generation. With her mother it had been emphysema.

Elizabeth's bathroom was cold. The slat window let in a lot of air. The strip heater above the bathroom cabinet didn't stand a chance. It was like trying to warm the ocean with a kettle full of hot water. As she read the instructions, Elizabeth remembered another test she'd done in a different bathroom, and the excitement that had followed.

If she and Charles were surprised at the results, it was nothing compared to her doctor. Pregnant, for the first time at forty-one: no IVF, no special herbs or diets. 'Remarkable,' he'd said.

'Call me old fashioned,' Charles had replied 'but I like to do these things by traditional means.' Elizabeth recalled the laughter in his voice. He would have made a terrific father.

Her morning sickness was debilitating. Morning, afternoon and evening Elizabeth felt nauseous. Even the thought of food made her queasy. Charles made dinner for himself and ate alone in the kitchen every night. It was only after the dishes were done, and all food cleared away that he would come to sit with Elizabeth in the living room, holding her hand while they watched television.

After two months the morning sickness suddenly stopped. Elizabeth and Charles were both relieved and celebrated by ordering pizza. Elizabeth even indulged in a small glass of red wine. But her next visit to the obstetrician brought terrible news. She still carried the guilt of having unknowingly rejoiced at the death of her unborn child.

'Chances are it was an unhealthy foetus,' the obstetrician said. 'The body deals with these things as nature intends.' He didn't need to tell them that at their age, another pregnancy, a healthy one at least, was unlikely.

It rained on auction day. Elizabeth huddled in the carport of the house with all the other would-be buyers. The well-groomed real estate agent was playing handmaiden to the auctioneer, who was clearly the one in charge. He wore a loud tie and a ridiculous red-faced grin. Elizabeth wondered where Helen and the rest of the family were.

'Since you're all shy I'll start the bidding at $900,000,' the auctioneer boomed, when things were slow to start. 'Do I hear nine-fifty?' Elizabeth had not intended to bid, but when no one else was forthcoming she raised her hand. 'Thank you madam, I have $950,000, do I hear one million?'

He did not.

It seemed Elizabeth wasn't the only sticky beak in the neighbourhood. The well-groomed real estate agent sidled up to the other people from her list, encouraging them to bid. Elizabeth watched as one after the other they shook their heads; then before she knew what was happening, she found herself being taken inside the house to meet the vendors.

'Your bid is well below the reserve,' said the auctioneer 'but you're first in line to negotiate with the owners. They're a terrific couple. She's an artist.'

'Is that so?' Elizabeth responded. Her heart was pounding. Surely they could tell she was a fake. But no, she was introduced to Henry and Helen and they shook hands politely. Helen asked if she'd like a cup of tea and Elizabeth said she would, thank you very much. Then she felt something move beside her.

'Hello,' said a small voice, 'friend of Mummy.' It was the little girl she'd last seen dropping breadcrumbs. At the time Elizabeth hadn't noticed the child's distinctive features, the eyes slanted upwards, the flat face and the wispy hair.

'Hello, I'm Elizabeth. What's your name Sweetie?'

'My name is Samantha, I'm six. How old are you Liz-beth?'

'Samantha, come and help Mummy in the kitchen,' Helen said.

'Bye-bye, I have to go now Liz-beth.'

'Good-bye Samantha, it was nice to meet you.'

The auctioneer began to speak even before the child had left the room. He told Elizabeth the house was worth one point two at least.

'I couldn't possibly go over a million,' she said. 'Most of my money is tied up in shares.' She stood up to leave, 'I don't want to waste your time.'

'Nonsense,' said the auctioneer, 'not if you come to the party and make a reasonable offer.' Elizabeth didn't like this talk of parties and she didn't like him, he was a bully. He reminded her of Charles's work mate who'd dropped off a box of her husband's belongings after the accident and then tried to sell her life insurance.

'Charles didn't have any and look how it's left you,' he'd said. 'You don't want to run the risk, now you know better.'

She wanted to say something about gates and horses bolting, but was struck dumb by his insensitivity. It wasn't long before the house was repossessed. Elizabeth missed the bathroom the most: the Italian tiles, the ducted heating and the fluffy towels. She still had the towels but they were faded and scratchy now.

In bed and in the dark, Elizabeth thought about her day. What an adventure it had been. She still couldn't believe she'd bid for the house, and met Helen herself and that sweet child. Then on the Monday, on her way home from work she noticed a *sold* sign on the board out front of the Johnston's home. Someone from the well-groomed real estate agent's list must have *come to the party*. She pictured the red-faced auctioneer dancing with his handmaiden and smiled to herself.

Elizabeth cooked a proper dinner that evening, meat and

vegetables. Afterwards she hung a towel over the rattley slat window and ran a deep bath. She found the stub of a dusty candle under the kitchen sink and secured it to a floral saucer with a dribble of hot wax. Elizabeth sat in the bath, warm and relaxed, watching the flickering light on the ceiling. Next weekend she would go back to the gallery that sold Helen's work, and buy a small etching of Samantha, if they had one. She'd reshuffle her budget. She could easily put off buying a new winter coat for another year or two. The holes in the lining weren't such a bother. She only remembered they were there when she found the tissues she'd put in the pockets, small and crumpled, following her like breadcrumbs.

Spouse Cycle

I am happily married, I am happily married, Norman repeats to himself. They say you can't choose your family but you can choose your friends; but after thirty odd years there didn't seem to be much choice in the matter. Norman couldn't really throw off Stevo and Jim now could he? I mean Stevo wasn't the sharpest tool in the toolbox. He could slam the front door in his face and Stevo would come round the back, with a six pack of beer and his stupid grin. Why Mary chose him over Norman back in year ten was a question that had plagued Norman for the better part of twenty years. So now she finally sees the light, dumps Stevo, and he's left consoling the bugger when what he really wants to do is console Mary. *No luck in life*, Norman thinks to himself. Still, he did alright with Steph, she's been a good mum to the boys and after what, fifteen years of marriage they still had some fun in the boudoir. But it's like eating Corn Flakes for breakfast every morning. Corn Flakes are good but after a while you feel like something different, a bit of Snap Crackle and Pop.

When Stevo gets dumped, Norman thinks, *I'm in with a chance.* Forgets his wife and two kids—just for a bit. He imagines making love to Stevo's wife Mary. She's got a bit more flesh on her than his wife Steph. Steph with her Pilates class, weight training and the rest of it. She's proud of her figure, his wife. He's noticed Jim eyeing her up on more than one occasion. *Help yourself*, he's tempted to say. If Steph strayed, that'd give him carte blanche, more or less. But Steph's not like that. She knows wrong from right. My God she didn't sleep with him for months after they started going together. That's what they called it back at high school: going together. He remembers Jim asking him, So you going together with Steph? It was during woodwork class as they were sanding down wooden spoons that they'd made for their mums, for mother's day. Spose I am, he'd replied. They had all hooked up young, not much else to do in a small town in the middle of the Wimmera. The rich kids were all in boarding school, meeting city girls. He, Stevo, Jim and their lot were left with the local girls. And happy to have them. At the time.

It was the floods that broke our marriage, Mary thinks. No, not broke: washed away. They stuck it out through the drought, but the floods were the straw that broke the conjugal bed. When Mary saw her life with Stevo washed away, she stopped to reflect on how quick it goes: life, that is. The hardest thing Mary had ever done was clean up after the waters receded. She pulled out mouldy carpet, swept mud out from the kitchen floor and picked up pieces of broken crockery. It was the good dinner set too, given to them by Stevo's parents for their wedding. Eighteen years on and she'd never used it—saved it for best. Like she saved most things. Mary had only ever been with the one bloke. She was almost forty and had only ever had sex with Stevo—that's when they had sex at all. He hadn't exactly been up for it very often during the past ten years. Stevo fell asleep in his favourite armchair most nights, after the six o'clock news. The nights he didn't, he was at the pub with the gang, Norman and Jim. He was more married to them that to her—felt like that some times. Mary told herself it wasn't important—the sex stuff that is. She told herself that Stevo still loved her. He often said he didn't know why she'd married him. But time was running out. Her chances of having a child were disappearing faster than rising flood waters. I'll be going through the change soon, she thought to herself, and I'll have nothing to show for my life. People had long stopped asking when she and Stevo were going to have a child. They assumed she was barren. They always blame the woman, Mary thinks. She'd done the same herself when Jim and his wife Susan stopped at one kid.

You can't leave me now, Stevo had said, I've just been diagnosed with diabetes. I need you to help me get through this.

The doctor told you to start exercising years ago, and he told you to cut back on the grog, she said. Stevo wept when Mary left him. She had never seen him cry before. Even at his dad's funeral, Stevo had been dry eyed. It was almost enough to make Mary stay—almost.

I am happily married, I am happily married, Norman repeats to himself, when Mary asks him to fit a deadlock on the front door of her new flat. She says, I asked Jim but he's busy coaching footy Friday nights. As soon as Norman walks in he wonders where the bedroom is.

Everything's new, Mary says. It's a fresh start.

Norman sees himself dropping into the flat after work. Doing it on the floor with fleshy, gorgeous Mary, right there in the small living room. No kids barging in, no toys underfoot. She has much bigger breasts than Steph—he likes that, yes indeed he does. Anything else I can do you for? he asks after the deadlock has been fitted.

Don't tempt me, Mary says. There's so much I'll need help with, around the place.

Wako the diddle-o! Norman thinks; then a second later, I am happily married, I am happily married, I am happily married.

Jim's worried. At the footy on Saturday, at his son's under eleven match, Stevo's wife Mary or rather Stevo's ex-wife Mary, put the word on him. At least he thinks that's what happened. Mary was there keeping his wife Susan company. But when she offered him a cuppa, he could have sworn she deliberately brushed her hand across his thigh and unnervingly close to the family jewels. He looked over at Mary and his wife Susan from the sideline. They were leaning on the hood of his Commodore sharing a thermos of tea. Both of them looked even heavier than usual in their puffy jackets. Lovely ladies they were, his wife Susan and Stevo's ex Mary, they both helped out at the fire station and volunteered with the elderly. The town couldn't survive without women like them—salt of the earth. But salinity could be problematic, particularly in regional Victoria. He wanted someone a bit more fun, someone who didn't see life as something to wade through; someone like Steph, Norman's missus. She looks about ten years younger than those two, he thinks, glancing over. Mary is looking straight back at him. Meanwhile, his own wife seems more interested in her hot beverage.

Truth be told he had a thing for Steph as far back as primary school. But he'd always been too shy to ask her out. She'd ended up with Norm, naturally. Norm played full forward on the school footy team, where Jim played the ruck. Well better that than Stevo, who couldn't kick straight if his life depended on it. Poor bloody Stevo, no wife, no kids, overweight and separated. Yes, life could be worse.

This would be the perfect time to get the band back together, Stevo thinks to himself. He has nothing else to do now that Mary has left him. Back in high school he'd bounced between two groups of friends, Norm, Jimbo and the footy guys, and Roger the drummer and his mates. In their heavy Doc Marten shoes and with their white shirt tails always hanging out, Roger and co were known as the weirdos. In the end he'd stuck with Norman and Jim. They were great blokes, real true mates. After his dad died he didn't know what he would have done without them taking him out of the house and to the pub of an evening. But now that Mary had left he didn't feel comfortable seeing the old crowd. They were all still married: Norman and Steph, the golden couple and Jim and Susan, the perfect couple with their perfect son. The kid was almost as tall as his old man—captain of the under eleven footy team and bowler for the cricket club. Jim was proud as punch, and so he should be, with a son like that. Stevo wonders what he's going to do with his old bass guitars once he's too old to play. He would have loved a son to hand them down to.

That'll be it for Stevo, Norman says to Steph, he'll probably never get laid again now Mary's left him.

Steph nods at her husband but thinks, I'd give him a ride. There was something endearing about Stevo. He was genuine, that's what it was. He was true blue, no bullshit—she liked that. Back at high school she'd had a secret crush on him. But girls like her didn't go out with guys like Stevo. Popular girls went out with popular boys, that's just the way it was. Steph had been slim, blonde, and she played netball—half the guys at school fantasised about her, she knew that.

She still looked bloody good for almost forty! As Norman gabbed on, Steph remembered watching Stevo on stage at the end of year twelve social. She was gripped by the relentless rhythm of his bass guitar—thump, thump, thump, it seemed to go right through her. It was like he was making love to her from the stage. Despite appearances, she had a feeling Stevo would be great in the sack.

And he's been told he has type two diabetes, on top of everything else, Norman says.

I might ask him to go for a run with me, Steph says suddenly to her husband. *Or get him into the gy*m. A bit of exercise would help stabilise his sugar levels.

Norman laughs out loud, Can you see Stevo getting off the couch to go anywhere other than the pub!

He needs some encouragement, Steph says, he needs his friends more than ever now Norman.

I've started running, Stevo tells Jim, with Steph. It was all Jim could do not to throw a punch at him, right in his dumb arse face.

What's her husband think of that? Jim asks.

Steady on! Steph and I are just mates.

'Course you are, Jim says, taking another gulp of VB. Perhaps I should pretend I have diabetes too, but I'm in much too good a shape to get away with that, Jim thinks. Now that he really looks at him, Stevo does look better. He's lost some of his beer gut, and he's drinking lemon squash! Jim can't deny that he's jealous, jealous as hell. How did dreary old Stevo land a gig jogging with Steph every morning? As if he didn't feel crappy enough. Just this week Jim's wife Susan had been diagnosed with breast cancer. The whole thing happened so quickly he hadn't had the chance to tell anyone. The two of them were leaving for Melbourne in a couple of days, where Susan was getting her right breast removed. Jesus! How was he going to cope with that?

Stevo stands at the door holding a bunch of flowers. Is Jim home? he asks when Susan answers.

Are the flowers for him?

Stevo laughs nervously. No, course not, they're for you. She was so brave, he was in awe of her.

Jim's just gone to fill the car with petrol, he'll be back in a tick, she opens the front door wider.

I won't come in, Stevo says, I just wanted to wish you all the best, you know, with the surgery. She looks nice in that brown jumper. He glances at her breasts. Stevo remembers Jim telling the gang about her. He'd just come back from his cousin's wedding in Melbourne— said he met a fantastic girl called Susan, who was studying to be a PE teacher. She's real down to earth for a city girl, Jimbo had said.

Funny he didn't mentioned how pretty she is, Stevo thinks when he meets Susan a few months later. He and Mary are already married by then. Susan was different from the local girls, though she fit in right away. His wife … his ex wife Mary and Susan had been friends from the get go. But then Susan made everyone feel comfortable. You could always put your feet up at Susan and Jim's place, nothing was so good that it couldn't be used. Not like his wife Mary and her bloody good china. She cried over the broken dishes more than she cried over their marriage. Jim was a lucky bloke, didn't know how lucky he was, really. Everyone knew he had a stupid crush on Steph. He looked ready to hit me, Stevo thinks, when I told him Steph and I were running

together. Silly bugger. Jim doesn't deserve Susan, he really doesn't.
Susan has always felt like an outsider in the group. The other five had
known one another since primary school. Close knit? More like tangled
threads. Truth be told, Mary and Stevo had been friendly from the
start—not as full of themselves as Steph and Norman. Poor old Stevo,
such a sweet man bringing her those flowers. He'll be lost without Mary,
Susan thinks. Mary was the one who wore the pants in that family. Can
a couple be called a family? We don't always get what we want, Susan
thinks. She would have loved a crowd of children, but at least she had
Jim Junior—quality over quantity. And her husband wasn't too bad.
Mary at least seemed a little taken by him. At the footy not so long ago,
she said, Your Jim's in good shape isn't he? Susan's never mentioned her
husband's temper, no point really, and it's only after he's had a few, and
then he's sorry right away—once he's sober. It's funny how he's not like
that with anybody else. She remembers last September when his footy
team lost the grand final. She can't remember what it was she'd said that
set him off. Jim lashed out at her face but accidentally hit her in the
breast. Then used it like a punching bag. Could that have anything to
do with the lump she found?

It makes you think, knowing you could be near the end. Makes
you think of what you want to do with what's left of your life. Susan
wonders if she should go to Melbourne for treatment on her own. Jim
probably doesn't want to come with her anyway. He's a coward when
it comes to hospitals and illness and death. And after her treatment
she will simply tell Jim that she isn't coming back, that she is staying
in Melbourne—for good. Her sister Joan has a spare room now that
her daughter has moved out of home. She could stay there until she
found a job and a flat of her won. Susan remembers what Joan said

the last time she ran away from Jim, I don't know how you can stand the sight of him, after what he's done to you. But Susan could never hate her husband. Without him there would be no Jim Junior. No, her husband wasn't that bad. Best leave things as they are.

I am happily married, I am happily married, Susan repeats to herself.

Tight Fitting

When Debra's husband was diagnosed with an aggressive form of cancer, all the mums at school were shocked and devastated. We instinctively put ourselves into Debra's shoes. Here she was, still quite young at thirty-five and with three young daughters that she'd have to raise alone.

The morning I found out about Debra's husband's prognosis, I wondered if any of us get through life without our quota of pain. Perhaps Debra had had it too easy. It was clear to see that she had always been popular, unlike myself who had never had a boyfriend until my mid twenties, and even then he wasn't much to look at. Debra had married her boyfriend from university. Geoff was tall, athletic and came from a well to do family. They married after a year of travelling through Europe together. Her mother-in-law treated Debra as a friend, and her father-in-law flirted with her. My in-laws were mountain villagers from a remote corner of eastern Turkey. They never approved of Stathi's and my marriage, forecasting divorce from the beginning. In that they were correct, which I suppose gave them some joy. They are cheerless people who live very small lives and I like them even less than they like me.

My children go to the same school as Debra's. It's an ordinary state-run primary school in a lower middle class area. Debra's living there has always surprised me. She and her husband seem more like private school types.

I suppose I was always a little bit jealous of Debra's perfect little family; of the fact she didn't need to work, even part time; of her suit wearing husband and of her three blonde daughters. But Debra's husband's illness changed that. I saw firsthand how easily everything in life, including life itself can be taken away and it frightened me. It frightened all the mums, and made us realise how lucky we all were, even those of us who work both in and out of the home.

And so at the first parent's association meeting Debra missed, when Geoff could no longer be left home alone with the girls, a few of us decided to set up a roster, to help out. My girls and I live just a few doors up from them, Stathi having moved out the year before; and so on mornings when Debra had to take Geoff to the oncologist or for treatment, I picked up her girls and took them to school along with my two. It made me feel good to be able to help in some way, and Debra was always very grateful, thanking me again and again. She was a lovely person and I felt awful that circumstances had made her life difficult.

In the last few months of Geoff's life, the dinner roster, which had provided family meals a couple of times a week, expanded to six nights a week. I took my turn with several of the other mums from school. I was known for my tuna pasta bake, and so I made that once a fortnight for Debra's family, sometimes varying it with extra veggies, and once with a feta cheese topping rather than cheddar. My in-laws had brought over a huge slab that they'd bought on special, and I didn't know what else to do with it.

After the first few weeks of this expanded roster it became apparent that ringing the bell and making even a cursory amount of chit chat was trying for everyone involved, and encroached on the family's privacy. I can only imagine how those little girls had felt having someone different turn up every night with their dinner. And so one of the dad's, Mike, built a wooden box with a sliding lid, which was positioned at the back door of Debra and Geoff's home. Food was dropped off here at 6.30 pm on the dot every evening. Mike's box worked a treat. I told him so at the next parent's meeting. I'd left the girls with Stathi, who lived only ten minutes away. Mike said it was the least he could do. Unlike my ex, Mike still attended school meetings, even though he too was divorced. I often wondered how his wife Judy ever let him go. He was a cabinet maker, good with his hands whatever the circumstances, I imagined. He wasn't very tall, though he would have towered over Stathi, but he was ruggedly broad, as was his accent. Yet there was a gentleness about him which I found very attractive. I stole glances at him during many a dull school concert and fantasised about asking him out. Some of the other mums picked up on this and I was teased about him mercilessly.

'Ask him out,' Trinh implored me.

'I just couldn't,' I replied, as we waited by the school gate for our kids to erupt out of the red brick building.

'I can see what you see in him,' Trinh said.

'Blind Freddy can see what I see in him,' I replied.

The week before Geoff passed away I had Debra's girls over for a sleepover. I told her I'd pick up her girls from school together with mine, and that we'd just drop in for a minute to collect their pyjamas and toothbrushes before going back to my place. Debra answered the door in faded grey track suit bottoms and an old t-shirt. I couldn't tell you what looked more tired, the fabric on the track suit pants or Debra's face. It broke my heart to see her like that.

The day after the sleepover Debra's in-laws moved into their house to be on hand. The girls went to school as normal through everything. Debra said she didn't want their schedule interrupted. Keeping things as normal as possible was a priority. I wondered how much the girls understood of what was happening. The youngest was in the same class as my six year old. I watched her leave school and run to her grandparents with a leap and a hug, smiling and laughing. The second daughter too seemed unaffected. It was only the eldest who carried her grief visibly.

There was an enormous turn out to Geoff's funeral. Several of the teachers from the school, as well as the principal, attended. They were a well loved family in our school community. I saw Mike standing alone out front of the funeral home when I arrived with Trinh and her husband and the four of us sat together. At one point in the service, Mike reached over and squeezed my hand and even in that sobering environment, I felt my ovaries twitch. A man like Mike would surely father me a son. I started daydreaming then, thinking that perhaps I would ask him out, after a few weeks, when things had settled down.

What is the appropriate length of time for mourning? My ex mother-in-law still wore black, though it had been eight years since the death of Stathi's brother Georgio, in a car accident. Of course it's different when a child dies, no matter what age they are. I first suspected something amiss when Mike and his boys sat with Debra and the girls at the school swimming sports. Needless to say she wasn't wearing black. She looked entirely too happy to me. In fact she looked better than ever. Her husband's death had rid her of a few extra kilos and she wore skinny jeans, like a teenager or a woman in her twenties. They were quite the *Brady Bunch*—she with her three girls and Mike with his three boys. It made me angry. 'No respect for Geoff's memory,' I whispered to Trinh.

'Life is for the living, I suppose,' she replied; which annoyed me no end.

Two months later, on my day off from the bakery, where I work during school hours, I was on canteen duty with Debra.

'I don't think I've shown you my engagement ring,' she said. She was wearing those jeans again. I wondered how she managed to sit down in them, they were that tight.

'It's lovely,' I replied, although *big* would have been a more accurate adjective.

'Mike and I don't want to rush into a wedding,' she said. 'We want to give the kids a chance to get used to our bigger family.' I managed a strained smiled. 'You were such an enormous help when Geoff was ill, I wanted to let you know before word got out.' I felt myself redden with rage and didn't trust myself to speak. I wanted to pull the ring off her finger and throw it across the room.

'What do you think of Mike?' Debra asked, like we were girlfriends at high school.

'He's very different from Geoff,' I replied.

'Chalk and cheese,' she smiled. 'But he makes me happy, and I guess I've learned that you have to take whatever happiness life throws at you.'

I'd like to throw something at you. 'Excuse me,' I said. I got up quickly, grabbed my handbag and walked to the toilet block behind the canteen. I sat down in my comfortable pants inside a cubicle and cried hot, bitter tears. Several minutes later the bell rang, and a moment after that I heard the sound of children running to buy their lunch. With only a moment's hesitation I splashed cold water on my face, put on my sunglasses and hurried out to the car park. As I drove away I couldn't help but think that the next hour was going to be murder with just one mum on canteen duty.

Steve's Sprig

A long time ago there lived an enlightened man called Buddha, who preached (amongst other things) the avoidance of accumulating material goods. His philosophy survives to this day and is known as Buddhism. This story, however, is concerned with an opposing doctrine, whose figurehead, Steve, once shared my apartment. Surely you've heard of Stevism? It has an authentic ring to it, doesn't it? Stevism—the cult of domestic appliances.

Some time ago I put an ad in the paper for a flat mate, and Steve replied. He seemed very nice. He didn't smoke. He had no pets. And he moved in within the week: he and his gadgets. I used to think the garlic press was a mechanical luxury. That is, until Steve moved in. The kitchen now had an electric can opener, electric knife, blender, liquidiser, microwave oven, cappuccino maker and small goods slicer. The only true luxury now was bench space. It wasn't long before the house was crawling with double adaptors and extension cords, a veritable circulatory system for the sustenance of Steve's electric organs.

In his room at night, he used an air revitaliser. I don't know why he didn't simply leave the window open and have saved himself four hundred dollars. And in the mornings his electronic alarm sounded through my wall. It was like a large van backing up over my head. I'd lie, wide awake, imagining and hoping it was a moving van—taking Steve away.

The hissing of the cappuccino maker would come next, accompanied by the vroom of the small goods slicer. Cappuccino and thin sliced salami on microwaved croissants—again. Couldn't he have had just a plain coffee once in a while? Steve's electric toothbrush vibrating the entire house signalled breakfast over, meanwhile my tea bags soaked silently in their pot.

Then there was his smugness! 'Why don't you use the toaster?' he'd ask me as if I were some kind of electricity shy Neanderthal. I'd shrug, and display what (imaginatively) might pass for a smile.

Apart from revitalised air, cappuccino, and thin sliced salami, Steve loved game shows which he watched on his large format colour television set. Every night I'd come home and find him in front of it, remote control by his side and feet up on his thermal massage pillow. He'd stay like that for hours.

I suppose what I hated most was the constant noise. From the time he moved in, in some part of the house, something would be beeping, humming, clicking, or vibrating.

Looking back I sometimes think it may have been easier to have simply asked Steve to leave. But all I needed for my enterprise was readily at hand. The electric knife worked beautifully. The microwave oven worked a treat too, and the liquidiser—they say human beings are 92% water. I used the shrill sounding small goods slicer on his you-know-what: and believe me, never had an appliance been more aptly named.

He isn't really gone. Steve's still here, but in the basement now. Liquidised, microwaved, and apportioned in a great number of various sized and shaped jars. Each has a little oil on top, and a sprig of mint, to keep him fresh. Same as the toothpaste he liked to use, on his electric toothbrush.

Symmetry

'One thing I do realise is that I'm getting uglier as the years go by.'

I turned to see who was talking. He was crossing the street as I was, walking beside me and a moment later, a step ahead. There were two of them, Asian students, boys with shiny faces, uneven skin. One was holding a stack of pizza boxes. It was strange to overhear a comment like that, which tied in to the very thoughts that I'd been having since 'celebrating' my 39th birthday. I had been thinking about death. I couldn't kid myself any longer, the halfway point was looming. Soon I would be falling over the cliff. Forget about knowing the moment of one's death. What good does that do? I was more interested in the half way point. Where the balance tips from growth to decay, from the best you'll ever be, to a slope of incremental but steady decline.

The strange thing is, he wasn't very old, the Asian student. Definitely in the first third of his life and yet his tipping point, according to him at least, had come and gone. Meanwhile I was travelling towards forty. I pictured a train speeding towards a ravine, like in a western. The track was broken and disaster lay irrevertibly ahead.

My name is Talia Brown and I am as strange as my name. Before people meet me they imagine a large African American soul singer. You know the type, built for comfort, exuberant, and with a voice to match. I am however white, petite and shy. And I can't hold a note to save myself. Here are some other things about me: I've had a number of flings but only one 'relationship'. Which, even at the time, didn't feel like a real one—the sort my friends were having. This quasi-relationship lasted less than six months and ended badly.

Some other things about me: I live alone in a one bedroom flat that I rent. I don't have a microwave, a mobile phone or a washing machine. I have never taken out an insurance policy of any sort and I have never owned a car. In fact my most expensive possession is my stereo: turntable, dual tape deck and speakers. Old school. I don't believe in music that is owned in megabytes. Mine fills shelf space and collects dusts. I have never been married, I have never been pregnant (let alone had a child), I have never eaten snails and I have never received a love letter.

I am half way through my life and I have nothing to show for it.

I had been on my way to the supermarket to buy sanitary pads when I overheard the 'ugly' remark. I am not on the pill and my period is irregular. The flow of blood caught me by surprise, and I was disorganised enough not to have any pads on hand. I looked in all the usual places, bathroom, laundry hamper, the third drawer of my dresser. In desperation I searched in my wardrobe. A tumble weed of discarded clothing rolled out, followed by a spare blanket, a stained pillow (in case of a not too fastidious guest) and a couple of handbags that were no longer in circulation. In a pocket, in the torn lining of a black vinyl backpack was one crumpled sanitary liner. It was like finding ten bucks on the street. The liner would see me to the supermarket.

While I was there I thought I may as well stock up and bought two packets of pads. My idea of buying in bulk is not a scratch on my mother's, who had walls of toilet paper in her laundry, and enough cans of beans and tomatoes in the pantry to see us through to the end of our lives in the event of radioactive fall out.

I could feel the liner quickly filling up as I navigated the aisles. The weight of liquid was making it heavy. The last thing I wanted was a leak, so I hurried to the checkout, milk and bread could wait until tomorrow. I put the two packets of pads on the conveyer belt and in an act of civic duty, placed the check out divider behind them for the next customer. That's when Jamie came to stand behind me in the queue. He put his packet of corn chips, chocolate bar and carton of milk on the conveyer belt, then glanced at my purchases, two packets of no-name brand pads.

'Hey, Talia. How's it going?' He must have thought I was a haemophiliac.

I'm menstruating, I wanted to say. I'm a fertile female of child bearing age. 'Fine,' I said. I had always had a thing for Jamie, although my best friend Sarah considered him a loser.

'That's nine forty,' the checkout woman said. I paid her in loose change and grabbed the grey plastic bag.

'See you round,' I said to Jamie; although this was unlikely, even if we did live in the same suburb. I wanted to run out of the supermarket, but took a measured pace and strolled off casually. I should have stopped to talk to him. How was I ever going to get into another relationship if I didn't even make an effort with guys I was attracted to? I was busy scolding myself when Jamie caught up with me at the crossing lights.

'Hey, I forgot to tell you about the gig I'm doing next Friday,' he said, reaching into his Crumpler bag and pulling out a wad of flyers. 'It'd be great if you could make it Talia.'

I read somewhere that the greatest sound to any person is their name, and that you can make someone like you simply by using it. People in business do it, sales people do it, and it seemed guys in bands desperate for an audience do it. 'Should be a good night,' Jamie said.

'Thanks Jamie, I'll try to make it.' Two can play at that game.

'Cool,' he said walking away in the other direction, then added, 'nice seeing you.'

I remembered the last time I'd seen him, it was the night we kissed, in a crowded hallway, at a party at Sarah's place. That was it for us, one brief encounter. I didn't give him my number, he never asked. That had been almost a year ago. For months I'd kept my eye out for him in the usual places and especially around home. I knew he lived nearby, but I never once ran into him, until now.

'He's a loser,' Sarah said the day after her party. 'He's never been in a relationship for longer than a few months and he's thirty-five.'

'Then according to your criteria, I'm a loser too.'

'It's different for women,' Sarah said, 'there aren't enough straight guys to go around.'

I had to agree with her there.

'Plus he's a drummer. He never even had the commitment to learn music properly, and that's something he's supposedly passionate about.'

'He's got amazing biceps,' I said, remembering his arms around me and how secure he made me feel.

'You're going to base a whole relationship on arms!'

It did sound silly when she put it like that.

There's something alluringly primeval about a man clubbing an object with a stick. A week later, as I watched Jamie on stage, I thought about cave men and their prey, and about stalking and hunting. I imagined Jamie pulling me by the hair into his lair and having his way with me—too many episodes of the Flintstones. I was transfixed by his powerful arms (enough already with the arms!). There's such passion in the physicality of playing the drums. Guitarists can pull all the strained faces they want during a solo, but for me the exertion and kinetic energy of banging on a drum kit is magnetic. As I watched him I remembered Jamie's kisses from the party at Sarah's house. There was definitely a spark between us. I finished my drink and got another. Whatever it took, I had to have him tonight. What was I waiting for I asked myself, to get uglier? The longer I waited the harder it was going to get for me to find a man. Of course by now it was the booze doing the reasoning. My brain was running on borrowed bravado.

'You OK?' Sarah asked. The gig was over and I was watching Jamie pull apart his kit and lug out.

'I know you think he's a loser, but if I don't go home with Jamie tonight I'm going to kill myself.'

'What's with you Talia? You're not yourself.'

'I'm sick of being myself,' I yelled above the noise of the crowd, 'I want to be someone else tonight, someone who has more fun, someone who gets what they want. I want a boyfriend and a regular fuck.' I stopped suddenly and Sarah looked as shocked as I felt. I never used the 'f' word. Either I was drunk or I was deadly serious. In fact I was both.

'I'm getting another drink,' Sarah said, 'but I have a feeling you've had enough.' She headed to the bar while I stood alone.

'So what did you think of the band?' Jamie asked. He was right next to me now, so close that I felt the humidity of his sweat soaked t-shirt. Before I could think, before my brain had a chance to veto my actions I reached up and pulled him towards me. I licked the moisture from his lips then opened my mouth and drank him in. I felt his arms around me and the dampness from his body merge into mine. I moved only an inch away and looked straight into his eyes, 'I thought you were amazing,' I said. And then I kissed him again.

When I awoke the first thing I thought was, how bad is my breath? I opened one eye and looked at Jamie, unshaved and with his hair ruffled he looked totally gorgeous. Then when he shuffled in his sleep and rolled over I slid out of bed, grabbed my top and undies from the floor and slipped into the bathroom, where I quietly cleaned my teeth and washed my face. Drool marks are seldom alluring and neither are crusty bits of (what is that substance?) at the corners of one's eyes. I looked in the mirror. The glow of sex suited me. It was a look I hadn't seen myself in for some time, but like a classic cut never goes out of style.

In the kitchen I put coffee on. I got butter out of the fridge and put some out to soften on a small Wedgwood plate—so much nicer than margarine out of a plastic tub. I found a jar of unopened apricot jam that my mum had made. If only she would soak the labels off: *Tahini - hulled stone ground sesame seeds*, it read. I transferred some into a glass bowl and put a teaspoon beside it. I set out cups rather than mugs and two matching plates, and I poured milk into a beautiful gold jug that I had found in an op shop. Then I sat down and waited.

'Morning.' He stood in the kitchen doorway wearing only his jeans. The sight of his bare torso made me catch my breath.

'Hi, you want some coffee?' I tried to sound breezy.

'I've got to get going actually.'

I tried not to look disappointed but the full morning-tea-at-the-Ritz spread belied my indifference. 'Never mind,' I said.

'I'll call you,' he said.

'Great.' But like last time, he didn't get my number.

Through the Window

Looking at Eric lying along the bench seat in the kitchen, Kerry couldn't tell if he'd passed out or was still conscious. Only last Friday she'd discovered that he slept with his eyes half closed. If I were a positive kind of person, thought Kerry, I'd say his eyes were half open. She didn't know whether to sit near him and hope for a repeat or ignore him. Their two flatmates Suzie and Harry knew nothing about what had happened last weekend, and Kerry felt it was best kept that way. Eric was only the second guy she'd ever slept with. Recently divorced, he drank heavily and carried a ton of Catholic guilt. 'Not exactly husband material,' she had written home to her sister the next day. Then added fervently 'Not that that's what I'm looking for!'

Tonight was Eric's birthday. He had said he didn't want to do anything, but people dropped by anyway and it had become another Nettleton Road kitchen party. Eleven people crowded inside four small walls, drunk and dancing under fluorescent light. The confined space heightened the atmosphere, concentrating the intimacy. There was not a corner to hide a clandestine kiss nor a nook to throw up in, not without everyone knowing.

Against the February-cold, the oven door was left ajar providing gassy soporific warmth. On one side of what had been a fireplace, shelves were stacked with pots that would never recapture their gleam, mismatched dishes, cracked tea cups and a pile of once white, now grey tea towels. Under the bottom shelf was a basket of potatoes and another of onions. Suzie's cat was in there, rustling the onion skins. The floor was wooden, bare, unpolished and gritty, the window panes dripped with condensation. The wall adjacent to the sink ran with tears of dried tea stains, where large soggy bags had missed the nearby bin. Perhaps because of their lax regard to domestic hygiene, the space was comforting; a place to put your feet up, where the kettle was always on the boil and the tea pot never had the chance to cool down.

Harry turned up the music. The small black boom box on the fridge buzzed. Reggae pulsed through the room, forming a conga line with the cigarette smoke. Harry and Suzie and their friend Jane were swaying with their eyes closed, each of them clutching a can of Tennents Strong. On a rickety chair a mate of Eric's carefully unwrapped some tin foil to reveal a small brown lump of hash. He proceeded to construct a dispensing device out of a drinking glass and a piece of cardboard. The mechanism confused Kerry who'd never been much good at science projects and had never mastered any form of drug inhalation.

Kerry looked over at her friend Rachel. She was sitting on some guy's knee, smiling a drunken smile and tipping back a can of Stella. Rachel was a fellow Australian, experimenting with foreign beer and foreign men, just as she was. Their hair colour matches, thought Kerry, then bottle-blonde guy sprung up to dance and Rachel's beer spilt all over her new jeans. She didn't seem to care, as he pulled her close and shuffled around the room—Fred Astaire meets Billy Idol.

'You OK?' Kerry asked Eric, touching his shoulder.

'I'm great, just great.' Eric replied with a lopsided smile. He had the look of a village idiot, really if she were honest, but his blue t-shirt highlighted his eyes, and all Kerry could think about was how much she wanted to kiss him again. It's all she'd thought about from the moment he left her room the Saturday morning before. Eric wore blue a lot. No doubt someone had told him that the colour suited him. It wasn't the sort of thing that would have occurred to Eric on his own. His attraction lay partly in his not caring, his effortlessness. His ex-wife would have had something to with it, Kerry thought.

'Can I get you some water?' Kerry asked, instantly regretting the motherly tone. Too nice, she admonished herself. Treat them mean, keep them keen.

'Kez, you are so sweet,' said Eric, then he sprung up violently and dashed towards the bathroom.

So sweet I make you puke.

Six months earlier, Kerry had arrived in London on a one year working holiday, looking for independence; something twenty-five years of living at home with an overprotective single mother and older sister made impossible. Her mother had been genuinely baffled at Kerry's decision to go to the UK. 'The weather is so much nicer here in Sydney,' she'd said. As if cloudless skies were what Kerry was looking for.

'We're a bit bohemian here,' said the blue-eyed guy who had answered the door. 'Name's Eric,' he shook her hand. She had come to view a room in a share house of artists. Well I'm interested in photography, she had reasoned, even if I am a preschool teacher. She followed him down the cluttered hallway past a rusty bicycle and a row of pegs holding an unrealistic burden of coats, cardigans and jackets. They reduced the width of the passageway by a third. Tumble weeds of dirt lay on the frayed carpet that bunched along the walls like an ill fitting jumper.

Kerry moved into the downstairs bedroom the following week and wrote to her sister, 'Mum would freak out if she saw this place.' The rest of London may have been living through the Greed is Good decade, but in the Nettleton Road house it was all about making art and music, drinking with friends and hating Thatcher. Kerry had crossed the globe to get away from her mother, but fate had found her another family in a corner of South East London. She marched in anti-poll tax demonstrations and drank at the local pub. 'Just like being in yer own front room,' said her flatmate Harry. Most nights he came home from 'the front room' on auto pilot. Kerry somehow felt like she belonged to this group of people and to this house strewn with dust and cat hair.

'Coming to Eric's gig?' Kerry's flatmate Suzie asked one Friday. They'd met on the front doorstep, Kerry on her way in from work and Suzie on her way out. All the way home on the bus Kerry had been thinking about taking off her shoes and sitting by the gas fire.

'It's only round the corner at the White Tavern, just put your jeans on, I'll see you there.' Suzie dashed off without waiting for a reply.

Eric's band were already onstage when she came in. Kerry got herself a drink then pushed through to where Suzie, Harry and some others were standing. Onstage Eric looked like a different person, and the music grabbed her from inside. God, he's amazing, she thought. She followed the curve of his lips, the outline of his slightly dimpled chin and metaphorically caressed his face. But it wasn't just that, his whole physicality, the way he stood, his long legs and broad shoulders, the veins that ran along his arms from elbow to bony wrist, outlined pale blue against his delicate skin; everything about him was painfully attractive. She noticed his hands for the first time, strong and large and playing guitar in a way she could only think of as quintessentially masculine. Then came a moment when he looked directly at her, from the stage, an electric moment so intense all time stopped and all sound faded away, or so it felt. Suddenly she knew she had seen the real Eric, seen beyond his cool facade. He was special, his music was passionate, poetic, beautiful. No wonder he didn't take his turn cleaning the bathroom.

The next morning Eric poured Kerry's cup of tea before his own, and flicked her playfully with the tea towel as they shared the washing up. In the days that followed he held her gaze moments longer. Kerry had always been cheerful, but Harry and Suzie couldn't help noticing she was especially sunny whenever Eric was around; and stranger still, Eric was helping with housework. For several months the terrace was an arcadia. Even the anonymous panda-eyed women leaving the house early in the morning didn't upset Kerry. She knew Eric wasn't seriously interested in them. She fantasized about the time when he would accept the obvious: that he was in love with her. He would move all his things to her room and use his room as a studio. 'We haven't even kissed,' she wrote to her sister, 'but it just feels like it's meant to be.' She imagined Eric telling her how beautiful she was, and how much he loved her. No one had ever told her she was beautiful.

Then last Friday Kerry found Eric in the kitchen, crying. She had never seen a man cry before. His divorce was through, and they'd all been to the pub to commiserate. He had seemed cheerful enough there, even buying an extra round of drinks at last orders. At home he put the kettle on and poured tea for everyone, like mother. Kerry took a cup to bed, an English habit she had adopted along with hot water bottles. When she awoke hours later to go to the loo, she found Eric alone in the kitchen, half-slumped over the greasy table and smoking. He looked up, his eyes were red, his voice choked.

'I'm twenty-seven next week Kerry, fuckin' twenty-seven and divorced. What a fuckin' loser.' She put her arms around him, as she had imagined doing so many times. The attraction was overwhelming; she couldn't have let go, even if a fire had broken out or the roof had blown away. When they kissed she felt herself merge with him completely, then wordlessly they walked to her room. He shut the door and looked into her face. 'You're everything I need,' he said. It was dark and she wondered if he could feel her skin flush under his finger tips. His hands caressed her cheeks, gliding down her neck and along the length of her arms. His touch was soft. As they made love he gasped, 'you're beautiful, I love you.' Kerry had never felt so happy, so adored. It's happened, she thought, moments before falling asleep, Eric and I are together. In the morning he kissed her on the cheek, thanked her for looking after him and crept back to his room. Since then they hadn't so much as shared the washing up.

Of course she told herself he was on the rebound, or rather at the point of impact. What did she expect? That he would get over his divorce in one night. No one's that good in bed.

'Come and dance,' said Eric's mate, Hash guy, who had disassembled his smoking device and was using the glass to swallow red wine. Kerry got up to dance but moved about distractedly. Her mind was on Eric, who'd re-emerged from the bathroom and positioned himself near the sink. Suzie and her friend Jane were there, rinsing out glasses. She tried to catch his eye, to get him up dancing, but his face was blank.

'Anyone for tequila?' shouted Jane, holding up a huge two litre bottle. Suzie was chopping up a lemon. 'Lick, sip, suck,' Jane chanted. Since that trip to Mexico she's like some kind of South American authority, thought Kerry feeling annoyed. Hash guy held her closer. She watched Jane and her Luna Park smile pour Eric a drink. Helplessly she danced with Hash guy, who swayed like a large lorry on a flat freeway. Moments later, on the bench seat, one metre away, Eric and Jane sat together, and they weren't drinking tequila. A sudden banging on the window startled everyone.

'Open up! I've been knocking on the front door for fuckin' ten minutes.' It was Gaz, the bass player from Eric's band.

'Hey man,' said Eric. The window squeaked open, letting in frosty air.

'I thought we were heading to Will's place tonight? I've got the lads in the motor out front, ya' comin' or what?'

'Yeah man, sure,' said Eric, putting a pouch of tobacco and cigarette papers in his back pocket. He climbed out the window without looking back, just a wave of his hand. It was such an Eric thing to do. Jane fiddled with her hair, straightened her skirt and rejoined Suzie at the sink. She whispered something and the two of them laughed. For a moment Kerry thought of following Eric. She had never left a room via the window before. But of course she didn't.

So, that's that, she thought. Well at least he's out of Jane's clutches. She tried to enjoy what was left of the party, but her mood had changed. Her friend Rachel and Fred Billy Idol Astaire took up on the bench seat where Eric and Jane had left off. Hash guy sat smiling at nothing in particular, and Suzie and Jane rejoined Harry on the dance floor, one square metre in front of the fridge.

Suzie's cat reappeared once most of the visitors left. Then Kerry put the kettle on and the remaining people crammed around the table, moving bottles and ashtrays to make room for hot tea. They discussed summer work in Spain, a friend's exhibition in Whitechapel and the bourgeoning romance between the Rastafarian mini cab driver from the end of the road and the red haired woman from next door.

Harry was in the bathroom and Suzie already in bed when Eric got home.

'Kez, this is Julie,' he said.

'Judy,' said the girl. She was young, maybe eighteen; wore no make up and still looked terrific though it was two in the morning.

'Tea's made. Good night.' Kerry couldn't wait to be alone and cry, really cry. He was just too damn good looking. She might have to move out of the house. It was different now that she'd slept with him. She couldn't bear this week after week. In bed she played out a different scenario, one where she followed Eric through the window, and went out with him and the lads. In her fantasy they came back home to his room and made love repeatedly. The picture was only slightly marred on reflecting, that in the entire time she'd lived in the house, she'd never once seen Eric's sheets hanging on the clothes line.

Kerry fell asleep eventually, but awoke not long after with a terrible taste in her mouth. She got up for a drink of water. Eric was in the kitchen, sitting in the same chair he'd been in the weekend before. When he looked up she was relieved to see he hadn't been crying. But he didn't look happy either.

'You said you loved me,' Kerry mumbled. She felt embarrassed saying it aloud but couldn't stop herself.

'At that exact moment that I said it, I meant it one hundred percent,' he paused. 'You know how fucked up I am.' It was a statement of fact and Kerry knew it. 'Besides, we're already living together, all that's missing is the piece of paper.' He smiled and she lost herself in a labyrinth of emotion. She smiled back, despite herself.

The next day Kerry wrote to her sister. 'Have decided to extend my work visa by another year. I've come too far to let everything go just yet.'

Cinnamon

1969

My name is Cinnamon, but that's not what I call myself. My name in Greek is Kanella, which means cinnamon. I was born in Carlton at The Royal Womens' Hospital. I'm in grade four at Northcote Primary school, my teacher is Mrs Taylor. At the beginning of the year when she first read the roll, Mrs Taylor said 'Kan-el-la! I'll never remember that. Can I call you something else?' Never mind it was my grandmother's name and her grandmother's before that, from the time of Alexander the Great. Dad says he conquered the world all the way to the subcontinent and introduced the spice to Europe.

I get called Katy now. I gave up my name, because if a name shows the world who you are, I did not want to be seen as different or difficult. But Kanella suits me. I have yellow-brown skin and long, straight, dark brown hair, which I wear in a pony tail. Of course in Australia everyone knows blonde is best. At school I look across the playground at the skips and wish I had lighter hair and a face sprinkled with freckles. I'm even jealous of their sunburn in summer.

We gather cross legged in the school hall to watch men walking on the moon, on a black and white TV. 'How marvellous,' says Mrs

Taylor. I don't understand her excitement at these unfamiliar pictures; after all, she flinches at the sight of my mortadella sandwiches. The thick cut bread, the meat that isn't ham. In the staff room they all eat neat, small, sandwiches and drink milky cups of tea. I take my turn with the other girls on staff room duty, emptying the tea leaves from the large aluminium pot and wiping up the scraps from the table into pages of The Sun newspaper. The teachers stand straight and are proud to sing God Save the Queen every Monday morning at the flag pole.

My best friend is Valasia, she gets called Val; she's lucky she can use her real name. Val lives next door to us. Mum says we're like gollos ke vraki, arse and undies, always together. I call her parents Thia and Thio, aunt and uncle. We're not related, but anyone from Greece is a relative of sorts, over here.

Someone is moving into the creepy old place next door to Val's. The grass and weeds that have grown through the diamond shaped wire fence have been trimmed back, so that the front lawn looks almost normal. The weatherboard house has been painted blue and the veranda no longer creaks when, as a dare, we run onto it, then dash back to the safety of the footpath. Val and I keep an eye on the place like the detectives on Homicide. One Saturday morning we see a family drive up: mum, dad and two boys. We rush over to help, even before they've started unloading their trailer. We both instantly fall in love with Robert, the oldest son. He's not Greek, but as Mum and Dad always say: Italian is second best.

It's summer and we're allowed to stay up late. Robert and his brother are playing cricket in the street with Val's brother and his friend Nick, rubbish bins for wickets. Sometimes Val and I are allowed to join in.

Afterwards we walk barefoot to the corner milk bar. Val and I jostle for position, both wanting to walk next to Robert. At Thio Yianni's shop we pool our money and buy twenty cents worth of mixed lollies: buddies, freckles, musk sticks and jelly babies, a multicoloured treasure trove.

Some mornings Val sets off for school early, without telling me; and I run to catch up with her and the boys from next door. I'm a month older, but feel small and out of focus. After school I stay indoors and read; and I haven't been to Val's place for dinner for more than a week. Mum says I'm *kria*, cold or standoffish. It seems I'm not outgoing enough to be truly Greek. Must we all wave our hands in the air when we speak?

At school, I'm having lunch with Toula when Val runs over. Not stopping to catch her breath she blurts 'Robert's holding hands with Suzanne White!' We run off immediately and see them behind the girls' shelter shed. Their hands are touching ever so slightly. This show of intimacy makes my stomach queasy. Val and I quickly re-bond, deciding his nose is too big anyway. We are determined no boy will come between us ever again. Along with Toula we imagine the scene when Suzanne's parents find out she's going out with a wog; we crack silly jokes and laugh until we feel sick.

1979

At university I wander around in a cloud of patchouli. I wear it behind my ears and on my wrists, and douse it on the hessian army bag I carry with me everywhere. It's almost impossible to be olfactorily distinctive. The union building reeks of dope and shaving one's armpits is optional.

I'm also aware of another odour I am exuding, or is it an aura, a confidence? I feel myself brightening, opening up to the world. I notice guys checking me out, and not just the creepy ones. Now I want to be noticed, to be exotic and decide to start using my real name. 'Kanella' everyone repeats. 'Where's that from?'

'It's Greek,' I tell them. 'It means Cinnamon.'

My best friend is Leslie, she's from Geelong and lives in the halls of residence. We look the same despite my brown hair and her reddish blonde. We both have perms to give our straight hair a bit of wildness, and both wear black kohl around our eyes for the same effect. We favour batik dresses or embroidered cheese cloth tops and gypsy skirts. Leslie carries a hessian bag just like mine and we're often found in the union gift shop browsing through dangling earrings and silk scarves.

University isn't for Val, she left school after form five to work for the local chemist. She helps old Greek people with their pills and lotions. They love her. I rarely see Val anymore, although I hear all about her from Mum. I still live at home, as a good Greek girl who isn't married should. But Val is set to move two blocks away with her brother's friend Nick and her new in-laws.

Val tells me she's pregnant the night her and Nick's families give *logo*, their word: a pledge of marriage. I'm shocked, I didn't even know she was having sex. The wedding is planned quickly but is still a huge affair. Three hundred guests and a bridal party of eight. Val's brother is best man, Nick's three sisters are bridesmaids. I'm sidelined, sitting on my parent's table like a child. Val's folks sit with their new *symbetheri*, in-laws, joking and laughing. One big, happy family. Everyone seems thrilled. I thought teenage pregnancies were frowned upon.

At my dad's name day party, ten months after the wedding, Val kisses me on both cheeks but we are no longer on the same side of the diamond shaped wire fence. My mother and all the other ladies fuss over Val's daughter Tess. They advise Val to have her next child soon. They talk about nappies, stubborn stains and breastfeeding. I sit quietly. I have nothing to contribute. My interests are watching *Countdown*, going to the pub and Mark from Biology class.

I have my first kiss on the final night of the Biology camp. As we sit around the fire drinking beer, Mark moves closer *to keep warm*, then makes his move. He is everything my parents don't want for me. He smokes, drinks and his engagement with multiculturalism is restricted to a love of Chinese dumplings. It doesn't matter, it's not like we're getting married. 'Divorce doesn't shame them,' says my mother. 'Their families are different from ours.' The week after camp Mark says *Hi* and keeps walking. In prac class he's at the other end of the lab. I write pages and pages in my diary nightly, documenting each encounter, every sighting around campus; and the number of times the phone rings at home.

Val's husband Nick wants to match me up with one of his cousins, also named Nick. Why not? I mistook Mark's drunkenness for intimacy. I'm nineteen going on twelve. We go to GOYA the Greek Orthodox Youth Association disco. They're all surprised I've never been here before. As Val and I wait for the boys to get back with our drinks, I realise I'm more comfortable when Nick is there and the distance between Val and I is less obvious.

On the multicoloured flashing dance floor Nick Number Two says 'Recon Katy's a better name than Kanella, why d'ya change it?' I can't be bothered explaining, especially to someone Greek. It's not the worst night out I've had, but I feel out of place, vulnerable and self conscious. My heels aren't high enough and neither is my hair. Contradictorily I can't work out if I'm invisible or whether everyone is looking at me. It's a question of focus.

In the back seat of the car on the way home, Nick Number Two lights up another cigarette. He smokes the same brand as Val's Nick. His aftershave too is oddly familiar. The combined aroma forces me to breathe through my mouth. I know this makes me look strange, but I don't mind. I dread the thought of Nick Number Two trying anything. As I press closer to my side of the car, I think to myself *Leave me alone, I am not one of you.* But of course everyone in the car knows this already.

1989

I am working at the Northland store of *Clear Eyes Optometry*, filling in for a colleague on leave. I'm normally based in the city. I am a professional woman with a twist. I wear smart black skirts and crisp white shirts with old men's vests, which I buy in op shops. I wear red lipstick and my hair is dyed blue black. Despite comments from short sighted Aussies, there is a marked difference between this artificial colour and my natural dark brown shade.

I'm grabbing a yoghurt at lunch time when I see Val's husband Nick with another woman. They are in the queue ahead of me at the supermarket. Is this what people who have affairs do? Go grocery shopping together? I can tell they are *together*. I'm not as naïve as I used to be. I've even moved out of home, into a flat of my own; well, that I rent. 'Throwing money away,' Mum and Dad say. Greeks never rent. Val and Nick have their own place in Doncaster now, a double fronted brick veneer with a triple garage. Greeks never buy weatherboard. Nick and the other woman only have eyes for one another and do not notice me slouching behind the fat guy ahead of me in the queue.

'Stop waiting for Prince Charming and just get married,' says my mother. I'm twenty-nine and considered an old maid. 'Too much education,' she laments. *Thia* next door agrees, she's glad Val didn't go to university. 'What's the point? She has a husband to look after her.' Nick and the other woman leave the supermarket. I have the same queasy feeling in my stomach that I had seeing Robert and Suzanne White together. Val's husband is cheating with an Aussie.

Mum has no idea that I have had a boyfriend for the last five months. She and Dad are not interested in boyfriends, only husbands. Neil moved into the flat downstairs from mine after splitting up with his wife. He is tall, blonde and recently separated: an Aussie with the lot. And he absorbs my every thought, every day, in a way that is exhausting. He's not the first, but my feelings for him are intense, blinding. He says 'You've helped me through a tough time.' I don't want gratitude, I want devotion. But Neil is far too preoccupied with his own problems to focus on my needs. The more I demand from him, the less I get; and the less I get, the more I want. We argue, then make up passionately: again and again. Mum and Dad think I'm militantly independent and don't want a husband, but the truth is I'm longing for someone that longs to be with me. And so, although I feel like I might fade away with grief, I decide to stop seeing Neil.

'I need you,' he says, turning up at my door with a mass of red roses. Passion is addictive and like any drug erodes one's will. The following night I turn up hesitantly at his flat. I know he doesn't want us to see one other every day and I'm nervous, yet have been compelled to go. But his face is cold, resolute and we quarrel publicly on his doorstep. Neil says 'I love you, but I'm not in love with you.' And with that he's heaved a blow from which I cannot recover.

I decide that I must go cold turkey and so move back home temporarily, telling my parents I need a break from some noisy neighbours. Mum makes my favourite meal, stuffed peppers and roast potatoes. Dad tapes *Oprah* for me to watch after work. Neil knows nothing of the strength of Greek families and the might of Greek womanhood. I have the backing of millennia.

I sit in my old room and wonder if my mother has been right all along: an excruciating thought. Perhaps I should marry someone Greek. But if a Greek husband comes with a guarantee, as my parents imply, Val should demand her money back. I'm not only miserable but frightened. One day I hope to have children and I want them to be born of an unbreakable bond.

1999

When I think of Ramesh, like the Cheshire Cat his smile always appears first. He is darkly handsome, cheerful and funny. I miss none of the angst and drama my life had before I met him. We met at a Film Discussion evening class and I knew right away that I liked him. During the first class, Ramesh backed me up when I made a derogatory remark about Bergman, then caught my eye and smiled. He sat next to me at the second class and we went for coffee together after the third. It was over two decaf lattes that he mentioned some reading he'd been doing. 'It seems the cinnamon tree is native to Sri Lanka.' His smile illuminated the entire room. That was five years ago. Ramesh calls me his Hindu-Greek Goddess. I've never felt so adored.

'I don't understand you,' says my mother. 'You've met someone black?'

'He's from Sri Lanka,' I tell her, 'but his family is Anglo-Indian.' To my parents they're all the same.

'How do you feel when we're lumped in with the Italians?' I ask.

'Doesn't bother me,' says Dad. 'Una faccia una razza,' one face one race, he quotes in Italian.

'He'll leave you for a girl his mother approves of,' says Mum.

'I might leave him first,' I say. 'You know how I hate to upset my own mother.' She smiles despite herself. Dad laughs and I get out the *kafembriki* to make three Greek coffees.

Ramesh's mother also has reservations. In many ways the two women are alike; holding their cultures close like life jackets, as they bob about in a country awash with difference. After our first meeting I asked Ramesh what his mother thought of me. I hoped I'd made a good impression. He moved his head from side to side in a hysterically funny imitation that left me gasping for breath. 'Goodness me Ramesh, she's darker than we are!'

We are at the Greek Orthodox church in Yarraville. Val's daughter Tess is getting married. Everyone is dressed to the hilt, men in suits, women in shiny fabric. Nick Number Two greets me with a kiss on both cheeks. His wife is slim and their four children are impeccably dressed. He tells me that they're all doing well at school and also Greek school.

Nick Number One comes to his daughter's wedding with the woman from the supermarket. Val is with her latest toy boy. Since the divorce she's lost some weight and looks years younger. She proudly tells me he's twenty-five and doesn't stop all night. I no longer even know what her favourite TV show is, and she's telling me this! I dare not look at Ramesh, I can just imagine the look he'll give me. I won't be able to keep a straight face.

Ramesh and I were married two years ago. We had a civil service. The Greek Orthodox church refused to formalise a union between one of its own and a non-Christian; so I wore a gold silk sari and Ramesh a white linen Achkan with gold buttons. We looked quite the pair. The celebrant on shift at the registry office was an ordinary looking woman called Rhonda. She read through the vows with little fanfare. My parents and the other Greeks had no idea what was going on. The Sri Lankans looked equally mystified.

The day after Val's daughter's wedding my mother calls to ask why I didn't join in the Greek dancing. I'm simply not very good at it, but she takes it as a racial slur. She says, 'Val and her two youngest are fasting for Easter,' no meat or animal products and adds, 'I wish you'd fast for Easter.'

'Mum! Ramesh and I are vegetarian, we don't eat meat 365 days a year.' She never dreamt her son-in-law would not be Christian. She must wish I'd married a plain old garden variety Aussie, someone to invite her and Dad over for barbeques.

'It wouldn't kill you to hold off on dairy products for a couple of weeks,' she retorts. 'Have you gained a couple of kilos?' I hope I've gained weight. I'd love to be pregnant. Ramesh and I stopped using contraception as soon as we were married. I'm thirty-nine and he's forty. At our age conceiving is somewhat in the hands of the

Gods. Luckily we have a plethora on side, from Zeus and Aphrodite to Shiva, Rama and Ganesh.

Postscript 2009

My daughter's name is Sophia, in Greek it means *wisdom*. Quite a name to live up to for someone still at primary school. I see Val with her grandson at drop off. He is in the same class as Sophia. They have told the other kids that they're cousins. I wave and Val smiles. I can tell she has something that she can't wait to tell me. Her eyes carry the same excitement I recognise from forty years ago. Life seems to have come full circle.

Acknowledgments

Heartfelt thanks to my publisher Gordon Thompson for his suggestions, enthusiasm and for his faith. Thanks also to my husband Craig, my parents Sophia and Panayiotis, also to Christina, Kosta, Margaret, Bethany, Rebecca, Lee McDonagh; and to my university superviser Brian Castro, who encouraged me to write funny.

About the author

Hariklia Heristanidis lives in Melbourne, Australia with her husband and daughter. She blogs daily at www.hariklia-what-she-said.blogspot.com.au This is her first published collection.